How God Used A
THUNDERSTORM

How God Used A
THUNDERSTORM
And Other Devotional Stories

Joel R. Beeke & Diana Kleyn
Illustrated by Jeff Anderson

CF4•K

© Copyright 2003 Reformation Heritage Books
Reprinted 2004, 2005, 2006, 2007 and 2009
Published by Christian Focus Publications
and Reformation Heritage Books
ISBN: 978-1-85792-815-0
Christian Focus Publications Ltd,
Geanies House, Fearn, Tain,
Ross-shire, IV20 1TW.
Scotland, Great Britain
www.christianfocus.com
email: info@christianfocus.com
Reformation Heritage Books
2919 Leonard St, NE, Grand Rapids, MI, 49525
Phone: 616-977-0599
Fax: 616-285-3246
email: orders@heritagebooks.org
Website: www.heritagebooks.org
Illustrations and Cover illustration by Jeff Anderson
Cover design by Alister Macinnes
Printed and bound in Denmark
by Norhaven A/S

Building on the Rock - Book Titles and Themes
Book 1: How God Used a Thunderstorm
Living for God and The Value of Scripture
Book 2: How God Stopped the Pirates
Missionary Tales and Remarkable Conversions
Book 3: How God Used a Snowdrift
Honoring God and Dramatic Deliverances
Book 4: How God used a Drought and an Umbrella
Faithful Witnesses and Childhood Faith
Book 5: How God Sent a Dog to Save a Family
God's Care and Childhood Faith

Acknowledgements

All of the Christian stories contained in these books are based on true happenings, most of which occurred in the nineteenth century. We have gleaned them from a variety of sources, including several books by Richard Newton, then rewrote them in contemporary language. Many of them are printed here for the first time; others were previously printed, without the accompanying devotional material, in a series titled *Building on the Rock* by the Netherlands Reformed Book and Publishing and by Reformation Heritage Books in the 1980s and 1990s.

Thanksgiving is rendered to God first of all for His help in preparing this series of books. Without Him we can do nothing. We would also like to thank James W. Beeke for supplying some helpful material; Jenny Luteyn, for contributing several of the stories; Jeff Anderson for his illustrations; and Catherine MacKenzie, for her able and invaluable editing. Finally, we would like to thank our loyal spouses, Mary Beeke and Chris Kleyn, for their love, support, and encouragement as we worked on these books over several years. We pray earnestly that the Lord will bless these stories to many hearts.

Joel R. Beeke and Diana Kleyn
Grand Rapids, Michigan

Contents

How to use this book

The stories within this book and the other titles in the *Building on the Rock* series are all stories with a strong gospel and biblical message. They are ideal for more than one purpose.

1. *Devotional Stories*: These can be used as a child's own personal devotional time or as part of family worship.

Please note that each story has at least one scripture reference. Every story has a scripture reading referred to at the end which can be used as part of the individual's or the family's Bible reading program. Many of the stories have other references to scripture and some have several extra verses which can also be looked up.

Each story has two prayer points at the end of the book. These are written as helps to prayer and are not to be used as prayers themselves. Reading these pointers should help the child or the family to think about issues connected with the story that need prayer in their own life, the life of their church or the world. Out of the two prayer points written for each story, one prayer point is written specifically for those who have saving faith while the other point is written in such a way that both Christians and non-believers will be brought to pray about their sinful nature and perhaps ask God for His salvation or thank him for His gift of it.

Each story has also a question and discussion section at the end where the message of the story can either be applied to the reader's life or a related passage of scripture. The answers to the direct questions are given at the end of the book. Scripture references are indexed at the back of the book. Beside each chapter number you will read the scripture references referred to. These include references within the story, question or scripture reading sections.

2. *Children's Talks*: As well as all the features mentioned above, the following feature has a particular use for all those involved in giving children's talks at Church, Sunday School, Bible Class, etc. At the end of the series in Book 5, you will find a series index of scripture in biblical order where you will be able to research what books in the series have reference to particular Scriptures. The page number where the Scripture appears is also inserted. Again, all Scriptures from stories, question sections, and Scripture readings are referred to in this section

It is also useful to note that each book will have a section where the reader can determine the length of specific stories beforehand. This will sometimes be useful for devotional times but more often will be a useful feature for those developing a children's talk where they are very dependent on the time available.

Shorter Length Stories

The following stories are shorter than the average story included in this book. They therefore may be used for family devotions, children's talks, etc. where less time is available:

Longer Length Stories

The following stories are longer than the average story included in this book. They therefore may be used for family devotions, children's talks, etc. where more time is available:

1. A Faithful Slave

Before the Civil War, there was slavery. People in the southern part of the United States had slaves who worked on their farms or plantations. Many slaves were treated well, although they had to work hard, but many other slaves were treated badly.

Cuff was the name of a young slave who was a Christian. He did his work cheerfully and was faithful to his master. But the day came when Cuff's master needed money and decided Cuff had to be sold. A young plantation owner, named John, who did not believe in God, agreed to buy Cuff.

When it was time for Cuff to leave, Cuff's former master said to John, "You will find that Cuff is a good worker; you can trust him. You will be happy with him, except for one thing."

"What's that?" asked the atheist.

"He will pray, and you can't make him stop. But that is his only fault."

"I'll soon whip that out of him," boasted John.

"I don't believe you will," said the former master. "I would advise you to leave him alone. He would rather die than give it up."

The young man did not answer. He was determined that the slaves should obey his rules. With a nod to the other man, and a shouted command to Cuff, they were on their way to Cuff's new home.

Cuff proved faithful to the new master, just as he had been to his former master. But John soon got word that Cuff had been praying, and Cuff was told, "You must not pray around here. Never let me hear any more about this nonsense!"

To this Cuff answered, "Oh master, I must pray to Jesus, and when I pray I love you and missus all the more, and I can work all the harder for you."

The master was unmoved. "I forbid you to pray any more!" he shouted. "If you do, you will be flogged!"

That evening, when the day's work was done, Cuff talked to God, like Daniel in Bible times. The next morning he was summoned to appear before his master.

"Why did you disobey me?" asked John.

"Oh master, I must pray; I cannot live without it," said Cuff.

At this the master flew into a terrible rage and ordered Cuff to be tied to the whipping post. Then John whipped him with all the strength he had, until his young wife ran out in tears and begged him to stop.

"Get back in the house," he snarled, "or I'll punish you next! Don't you dare interfere in my affairs!" He continued to whip Cuff until he was exhausted. Then he ordered Cuff's bleeding back to be washed in salt water before the slave returned to work. Do you think Cuff was angry with his cruel master? Even though he was in terrible pain, he went away singing in a groaning voice:

My suffering time will soon be o'er,
When I shall sigh and weep no more.

Cuff worked all that day, as the blood oozed from his back where the lashes had made long, deep furrows. But God was using this for good. All day long, God was working in the master's heart. John's eyes were opened to his wickedness and cruelty. The master was learning that what he did was wrong. In great distress he went to bed, but could not sleep. His agony was so great that at midnight he awakened his wife and told her he thought he was dying.

"Shall I call the doctor?" she asked in alarm.

"No, no. I don't want a doctor."

His wife looked confused. "I don't understand."

Shame covered the young man's face. "Is there anyone on the plantation who can pray for me? I am afraid I am going to hell."

"Nobody," answered his wife, "except the slave you punished this morning."

John was silent then he asked anxiously, "Do you think he would pray for me?"

"Yes, I think he would," she replied.

"Well then, send for him quickly."

The servant found Cuff in his hut on his knees in prayer, so Cuff was sure he would be punished again. But when he was brought into the master's bedroom, he saw that his master was in great distress. With a groan, John asked, "Oh Cuff, will you pray for me?"

"Yes! Bless the Lord, master, I've been praying for you all night," exclaimed the faithful slave. He dropped to his knees, and like Jacob, he wrestled in prayer. The Lord was pleased to hear Cuff's prayers, which were soon joined by those of both master and mistress. The night was spent in prayer and the reading of God's Word. God the Holy Spirit worked a change in the hearts of the young man and his wife. Master and slave embraced. Past cruelty was forgiven, tears of joy were mingled, and the angels in heaven rejoiced.

In the days and weeks to follow, the young couple and Cuff spent much time studying the Bible and praying, for they had much to learn. Cuff was set free, and worked no more on the plantation. Later on, John took Cuff and together they went out to preach the gospel. They traveled all over the south, witnessing to the power of Christ to save completely and forever.

"Herein is love, not that we loved God, but that he loved us, and sent his Son to be the propitiation (satisfying sacrifice) for our sins" (1 John 4:10).

Question: Are you a good example to others? Do you pray for your enemies?
Scripture Reading: 1 Peter 2:18-25.

2. A Gentle Spirit

Several men were visiting at a friend's house. The men sat in the living room. At the dining room table sat Seth, doing his homework. He liked to listen to the men's deep voices, and had promised his father that if the men's conversations became distracting, he would take his books upstairs and work in his bedroom.

Seth was hard at work when one of the men said something that caught his attention.

"A gentle spirit is a cure-all, I always say," the man said.

Wondering what it could mean, Seth repeated the statement aloud. "A gentle spirit is a cure-all."

Seth had not counted on being overheard. He was a shy boy, and was very embarrassed when the men looked at him.

"That's true, young man, don't you think so too?"

Seth went over to his father, finding security at his father's side. "I don't know what it means," confessed Seth shyly.

The man smiled at Seth and patted his arm. "Well, then, I'll have to tell you what I mean. It's very important to know that a gentle spirit is a cure-all. I think the best way to explain it is to tell you how it changed me.

"My father was an officer in the army, and he thought the best way to settle everything was by fighting. If a boy teased me, he would tell me to fight him to teach him a lesson.

"My parents sent me to a famous school. Next to me sat a boy named Tom. When I found out that he was poor, and lived in a run-down home, I became proud, and told him about my father, the officer, and what a nice home we had, and the toys I played with.

The man paused and shook his head, and then continued. "Tom was a good student though, and everybody liked him. He was also good at playing baseball, so, for a while we got along quite well.

"But one day, another boy and myself got into trouble at school. Someone told me that Tom had told the teachers what we had done, and that was why we now were being punished. I was furious. After school, I went to Tom's house. I was planning to teach him a lesson. I found him in his yard, playing with his little sister and their dog. I yelled at him, 'I'll teach you to tell the teachers on me, Tommy Tattle Tale!'

"Tom just stood there looking at me, gentle as a lamb. He wasn't scared of me at all.

"'Did you tell the teachers on me?' I shouted. 'Tell me, or I'll hit you!'

"Tom stepped aside, and said firmly, 'You may hit me, but I want you to know that I won't fight back. Fighting is not the way to solve problems. When you are cooled down, I'll talk to you about it.'

"I was very surprised. And of course, there's no fun in having a fight if the other boy won't fight back. He was so firm, but yet so mild! I felt ashamed of myself. My anger evaporated, and I left feeling foolish. Tom had actually won the fight without fighting. From that day on, I had respect for Tom. He taught me that a gentle spirit is a cure-all. It changed my thinking. Never again did I think fighting would help me. God used Tom to teach me that fighting is sin. God's gentle Holy Spirit washed me and cured me."

Question: If someone is cruel to you, how should you respond? What did Jesus do for those who hurt Him on the cross? In Titus 2:12 & 13 we are told how to live a virtuous, godly life. What do you have to deny and what do you have to do?

Scripture Reading: Leviticus 19:17&18.

3. An Enemy in Disguise

Hugh, a brave young soldier, announced, "I will stand guard tonight." A shocked silence followed his announcement. They were fighting a war with the Indians and on each of the four previous nights, the guard on duty had been killed. Now Hugh had offered to take the dangerous position of guard for that night. At last one of his friends spoke. "You will be number five!" he said, breaking the stunned silence.

"Oh, don't worry," Hugh replied. "I have orders to shoot anything that moves, and you can be sure that even if it is only a bird, I'll do it!"

That night as he stood guard, Hugh could not help picturing the faces of his four dead friends. His senses were very sharp as he realized the great danger he was now in. His post was on a small hill, and between him and the distant forest was a stretch of partially cleared land. Hugh remained alert through the long hours of the night but no sign of life broke the stillness.

As dawn began to steal across the sky, Hugh almost felt disappointed that nothing had happened to share with his friends. At the same time he idly watched as a wild hog left the safety of the forest. It seemed to be picking up food as it gradually came closer. Hugh paid little attention to the animal until, when it was quite close already, he remembered his orders to shoot anything that moved.

"Well," he thought, "I must follow orders, even though the beast is hardly worth the bullet."

The sharp cry of a wounded Indian broke the stillness which brought two other soldiers running to the spot. They discovered that an Indian had cleverly disguised himself as a wild hog and had nearly succeeded in coming close enough to kill guard number five.

Hugh was filled with deep gratitude and thankfulness to God when he saw how narrowly he had escaped death. He had been saved by the wonderful providence and mercy of God.

Question: This story of natural war can be used as an example of spiritual warfare in the hearts of God's children. Who is our enemy? Why must we be on our guard all the time to fight against all sins and temptations?
Scripture Reading: Genesis 3.

4. Beware of Bad Friends!

Once again Bill had gone down to the docks to see Sam Jones. He knew his mother was probably worried about him, but Bill was becoming more and more attracted to Sam's invitation to go to sea.

Sam was a wild boy with rebellious ideas who often used rough language, but he told Bill of the wonderful things he had seen in far-away lands. "Come on, Bill," he urged. "My dad is the skipper and I know he will take you. Think of how much fun we could have together!"

"But mother won't let me go," Bill answered. "Besides, Captain Downe says I'm too young."

Sam's reply was an oath filled with rough language. Yet Bill would not admit to himself that Sam was bad company for him and kept visiting the docks in spite of the warning voice of his conscience.

At home, Bill told his mother, "I want to go to sea. Sam's father is willing to take me on."

"Oh, Bill!" his mother cried. "You are all I have. I cannot part with you yet!"

"I'll have to go sometime," Bill grumbled.

He refused to think about his mother. She was a widow and in poor health. She needed all the love and support he could give her. But that interfered with his longing to go to sea with Sam. This made him unpleasant to his mother and he would often answer her roughly or not do what she asked. His mother became very worried, and brought her concerns before the Lord. She often prayed, "Lord, I am afraid that Bill is under evil influences. Please keep my boy from going astray."

One Saturday evening Bill sat up late watching his mother. "Oh, Mother!" he said. "All you do is stitch, stitch, stitch! You will wear yourself out."

"I don't mind as long as you are here," she replied smiling.

Bill shut his book and went to bed. "If only I could go to sea," he muttered, "at least I could earn something so she would not have to work so hard."

The next morning Bill awoke with the warm sun shining down on him and the clean clothes which his mother had laid out for him. How fresh and neat they looked; and there, too, was his mother's work from the previous night, a new shirt which she had finished for him to wear to church.

"How good and dear mother is!" he exclaimed, and again his eyes returned to the clothes. Somehow they brought out his mother's love and care as never before. In a wonderful way Bill's heart and conscience were touched. Tears filled his eyes – not proud, angry, rebellious tears because he could not have his own way – but sweet, penitent tears for grieving such a love as hers. "I will never, never hurt her by going to sea, or even mentioning it again," he decided, and he kept his promise.

Not long after this, he went to work for a carpenter. One day Sam Jones came to see him. In his usual rough language, he told Bill that he had found a place for him. "You must come now," he said. "Run away tonight."

"No," said Bill. "My duty and decision is to stay at home with my mother and that is final." When Sam saw that Bill's mind was made up, he went away. It was not hard for Bill to get rid of bad company once he decided to.

A year later, Bill's mother died. He felt that he could never thank God enough for speaking to his conscience on that sunny, Sunday morning, and keeping him at home! It had been the beginning of the best year of his life, when he was happy doing all that he could for his dear mother.

Question: What does the Bible say in Exodus 20 about those who honor their parents? What will happen to them? What does Colossians 2:8 warn us about?
Scripture Reading: Proverbs 1:8-19.

5. Bless and Curse Not

Sally was seven years old and loved Jesus. She memorized a verse of Scripture every morning, and recited it to her mother before school. Sally's father, however, was very wicked. One morning he swore at his wife. Then Sally came in and said, "Mamma, I know my text. May I say it now?"

"What is the text, my dear?" asked her mother, wishing to keep the child from hearing her father's terrible oaths.

"Bless and curse not" (Romans 12:14b) was the text. As she spoke, she went to her father for a kiss before she left for school. The father soon left for work, but could not forget the words he had heard. Wherever he went, "Bless and curse not" rang in his ears. He became a changed man. Cursing was no longer heard from his lips. Scripture and repentance now flowed from his tongue. Later, because of God's saving work, he sang songs of deliverance and thanked God for his precious daughter.

Question: What scripture verse in Exodus 20 tells us not to use bad language?
Scripture Reading: 1 Corinthians 4:11-16.

6. Fighting Against Sin

Marian had a little brother named Benny. Benny had a bad temper. When he was angry, he would hit and kick. Benny was always being punished for his bad behavior. One day, Benny hit Marian. Their mother was going to punish Benny, but Marian said, "Mommy, don't punish him this time. I think I know how to teach him not to hit anymore."

She took Benny out of the room. The mother followed to see what Marian would do. The girl went into another room and closed the door. She made Benny kneel down by a chair. Then she knelt down beside him, and prayed a simple prayer. "O Lord, forgive my little brother for hitting me. Give him a new heart so that he won't hit me anymore; and if he does hit me or push me, help me not to hit him back. Help me to be patient with him. Lord, hear me for Jesus' sake. Amen."

Question: What is your first reaction when someone hits you? What should you do when someone is nasty to you?
Scripture Reading: Luke 6:27-38.

7. Forgiveness

Danny Reynolds had one great trial in his life. He attended a boarding school in England, which meant that he stayed there day and night, and did not come home until summer time. This was much more common a long time ago, since people were not able to travel as easily as we do today.

Danny loved his teachers, and most of the boys in his school were good-natured and kind. But there was one boy who constantly teased and annoyed everyone in the school. His name was John Ferguson. John sat next to Danny at school, since they were in the same class, and they shared the same bedroom.

When Danny wrote to his mother, he would tell her how much John teased him and whispered mean things to him in class. John often made fun of Danny in front of the other boys, and when the teachers were not looking, he would kick Danny, or trip him, or knock his books out of his hands. Danny thought that nobody was teased as much as himself. He would cry when he wrote to his mother. He told her that he prayed about it, but the Lord did not seem to hear him, for nothing changed.

Time and again, Danny's mother would encourage her son in her letters, advising him to practice the golden rule of returning good for evil, and win John's heart by kindness and love. She reminded Danny of the lesson Jesus taught his disciples when Peter asked, "How oft shall my brother sin against me, and I forgive him? till seven times?" (Matthew 18:21). Jesus' answer was a surprise for Peter: "Until seventy times seven." The Savior then told the parable of the unforgiving servant. You can read it for yourself in Matthew 18:21-35.

But forgiveness is not easy to practice, and poor Danny often found it very difficult to do his best to be loving, kind, and forgiving.

But the Lord did hear Danny's prayers, and those of his mother. The Lord always hears prayer, but He answers in His own time and in His own way. One day, John Ferguson became ill. As he lay on his bed, he began to think about his mean and selfish behavior toward the other boys at school, and especially toward Danny Reynolds. His conscience bothered him; but something else bothered him too.

John had some canaries for pets. He loved those canaries very much, and always took good care of them. Just this week, they were sitting on their nests, which meant that soon little birds might hatch. It also meant that the canaries needed special care and attention. John did not dare ask anyone the favor of helping him. Only last night, John had tormented Danny's pet rabbit by locking it up in a box for several hours. When Danny finally found the rabbit, it was terrified and exhausted.

John didn't dare ask Danny to look after his canaries now, and he believed Danny was the only boy who would even consider helping a mean boy like himself. He was too proud to apologize to Danny, so he fretted and worried about his canaries.

Day after day passed, and John was still sick, but still he did not ask Danny to help him care for his birds. Danny, however, understood how much John loved his canaries. He had seen him talking to them and carefully feeding them. He also knew that they needed special care at this time. But Danny kept thinking of what John had done to his poor rabbit, and he was tempted to neglect John's canaries, just to get back at him.

But Danny's conscience would not be quiet. The words of Jesus, "until seventy times seven," stayed in his mind as he stood by the canaries' cage when he had finished caring for his rabbit.

"Lord Jesus," prayed Danny, "this is very hard for me to do. Sometimes I feel like I hate John. He's always mean to me; he's never done one nice thing for me!" Tears formed in the little boy's eyes. "I know I have to forgive John, and that I should care for his birds, but I need Thy help. Give me Thy Holy Spirit in my heart; give me Thy grace; pray for me, Lord Jesus! Help me to forgive John, and help me to do this cheerfully. For Jesus' sake, Amen."

Danny smiled then. With the Lord to help him, he would do it. So, without John knowing anything about it, Danny cared for those canaries as if they were his own.

Two weeks passed before John was better. When he was able to visit his canaries, he was so surprised to find the cages clean, and the five little birds healthy and well cared for! Without question, Danny had done this for him. This thought tugged at his conscience. Would he have done the same for anyone else? John began to see how very selfish and mean he had become.

After this, John was not quite so mean as before, but his heart was not changed. He was still selfish, and still teased and annoyed people, although not as badly as before. Danny was very disappointed about this, and wrote this to his mother. Mrs. Reynolds encouraged Danny to keep praying for John, and to keep asking the Lord to help him forgive "till seventy times seven." She told her son that she prayed for Danny and for John every day, and reminded him that in a few weeks it would be summer vacation and he would be home for several weeks.

This made Danny happy. In a few weeks he would be going home. He could hardly wait! But then came some troubling news. John had received a letter from his family, which told him that he was not allowed to come home for the summer. His whole family was very sick with a fever, and they did not want John to catch it. The doctor said it was best for John to remain at the boarding school. John, of course, was very disappointed. He had looked forward to going home for the summer, and now he would not be able to see his family.

John was not the only one affected by this news. Danny was sad too, not really for John, but for himself. He knew what God wanted him to do. It was a hard struggle, and Danny prayed earnestly to the Lord to help him with his difficult choice.

"Lord, help me! I don't want to do this! I need Thy help again. I know what I have to do, but it's the hardest thing I've ever had to do, Lord. Give me love and forgiveness and compassion. For Jesus' sake, Amen."

Then Danny dried his tears, sat down at his desk and wrote his mother a letter asking her permission to bring John home with him for the summer vacation. When his mother gave her consent, Danny went to tell John. You can imagine how surprised John was! He had not expected this kindness. He had been dreading a long, lonely summer at the boarding school. At last John's hard heart broke, and he shed tears of repentance. He asked Danny's forgiveness for the cruel things he had said and done to him. John also asked God's forgiveness, confessing his sins and asking the Lord for grace and mercy.

Danny had been dreading the summer, but it turned out to be a summer both boys would remember for a lifetime. John found forgiveness in the blood of the Lord Jesus Christ, and Danny learned that following his Master was best, even if it is difficult.

Children, there are many lessons to be learned from this story. Perhaps some of you are teased at school, or perhaps the Lord has placed other difficulties in your path. Ask the Lord to teach you the lessons of forgiveness, repentance, and faith in the Lord Jesus Christ. Always remember that the Lord will help you and bless you when you walk in His ways. Remember to ask the Lord for His help every day, and for the desire to do what He wants us to do. We need His help for everything.

Perhaps there are some of you who tease other children. This is a terrible sin. Do not think for a moment that the Lord does not see it. Not only do you cause the other child much pain, but you also hinder your own salvation. "If I regard iniquity in my heart, the Lord will not hear me" (Psalm 66:18). In our story, John was forgiven by the Lord and by Danny and his mother, but I am sure he was troubled by these painful memories for the rest of his life. Dear children, flee with all your sins to the Savior, and He will make you clean. He has promised salvation and forgiveness to those who come to Him confessing their sins. That includes all of you. I think that those of you who are teased often respond in anger and with mean words, rather than with Danny's prayerful kindness. "If we confess our sins, he is faithful and just to forgive us our sins,

and to cleanse us from all unrighteousness"
(1 John 1:9). Go to Christ, children, and you
will find a faithful, loving, forgiving Savior.

Question: Who has God promised salvation
to? Who forgave John in the story?
Scripture Reading: Matthew 18:21-35.

8. Help with School Work

Steven was a good student. He always did his best, but some things were hard for him. For instance, today the grammar lesson was very difficult. He had listened to the teacher's explanation, and even gone to her for help, but still Steven did not understand the lesson.

"Take your book home with you tonight, Steven," smiled the teacher. "Study it at home, and you will discover that it's not so hard after all."

Steven felt very discouraged. Now he had lots of homework. But perhaps his mom and dad could help him understand it.

While Steven ate his after-school snack, he told his mother about the difficult lesson. "I tried and tried, and I just don't get it, Mom!"

"Let me help you then, Steven," offered his mother.

His mother did her best to help him, explaining the parts of a sentence, and all about nouns, verbs and adjectives. But Steven grew more and more confused.

Finally he pushed his book away and said, "I'll be back in a few minutes, Mom."

Soon Steven was back. Gone was the frown of frustration, and in its place was a happy smile. "All right, Mom. I'm ready now! I asked God to help me understand it. He always helps us if we ask Him, so I'm sure if you explain it one more time, I'll understand it."

Mother and son bent over the book one more time. One more time, Mom explained the assignment to Steven. And Steven, expecting the Lord's help, was not disappointed. With the Lord's help, Steven was able to understand the lesson, and do his homework easily.

Children, you must also ask the Lord for help in everything. He is ready and willing to help you in every area of your life. You cannot do without the Lord's help. David spoke often of the Lord's power and willingness to help. Here is one text: "Commit thy way unto the LORD; trust also in him; and he shall bring it to pass" (Psalm 37:5). Trusting in the Lord should be your way of life.

Question: Have you learned to trust only in the Lord? God is powerful enough to help you. Is He willing to help you?
Scripture Reading: Philippians 4:4-9.

9. Learning to Pray

Once there was an old man who often said that he never went to bed without saying the prayer his mother had taught him as a little boy. He was pleased with himself, because he thought his prayer pleased God.

One Sunday, he went to Sunday School. The teacher asked what praying meant. One little boy answered, "It's begging from God."

The old man was startled. He had never thought about prayer in that way before! He kept thinking about the little boy's answer and the Holy Spirit convicted the old man. When he got home, he fell on his knees, but this time he did not say the prayer his mother had taught him. With tears rolling down his cheeks, he confessed that he had never truly prayed and begged forgiveness for Christ's sake.

Do you think the Lord forgave him? Yes. After that, the old man would tell people, "I am the old man who said his prayers for seventy years, and never truly prayed until the Lord taught him how!"

Question: For what did the old man beg God in Jesus' name?
Scripture Reading: Matthew 6:5-15.

10. Praying Soldiers

Queen Wilhelmina of Holland once paid a visit to an army unit in 1914. She believed that the strongest army to defend their country would be a praying one. She therefore asked a soldier, "Who of you pray?" She did not ask, "Who can fight well?" or "Who is brave?" She asked, "Who of you pray?"

All eyes were on the queen; no one had expected this question. They could fight, gamble and swear, but pray? Most would have felt ashamed to pray. But the queen was asking who among them prayed.

At last, eight young men were found who acknowledged that they prayed. The queen spoke again. "Such soldiers are worth more than all the others," she said. "Such soldiers can defend our country." She then requested the soldiers to sing from Psalm 79:

> Help us, God of our salvation,
> For the glory of Thy Name;
> For Thy Name's sake
> Come and save us,
> Take away our sin and shame.

Question: Why did the queen think that a praying soldier was stronger than one who did not pray?
Scripture Reading: Exodus 18:18-20.

11. Simple Trust

Nancy was an old woman who lived in Scotland long ago. She had been a God-fearing woman for most of her years. Her home was a lowly thatched cottage in one of the quiet glens of Scotland. Now she was sick and was quietly waiting for death to end her sufferings and to take her into the presence of the Savior who she loved. By her bedside on a small table lay her glasses and her well-thumbed Bible. She called it "her barrel and her cruse", for, she said, it had never failed her, and she had fed continually on the "Bread of Life".

A young man in the village often came to see her. He was a Christian in name, but not in his heart; he did not understand Nancy's love of God's Word. God was not real to him. Yet he loved to listen to her as she talked of her precious Savior. When she spoke of her home in heaven, it seemed very near. The young man was drawn by Nancy's faith. One day he put this startling question to the happy saint: "What if, after all your watching and waiting and prayers and hopes and expectations, God should permit your soul to be lost forever?"

The faithful old Christian raised herself on

her elbows, laid her right hand on her precious Bible, which lay open before her, and turning to look earnestly at the young man, she quietly said in her thick brogue, "And is that a' ye know aboot the Bible, mon?" Then, her eyes sparkling with heavenly brightness, she continued, "God would hae the greater loss. Poor Nancy would only lose her soul. That would be a great loss indeed; but God would lose His honor and His character. Haven't I hung my soul on His 'exceeding great and precious promises'? And if He should break His Word, He would prove Himself untrue and a' the universe would rush to ruin!"

How simple! How scriptural! How touching was the confidence of that dear old child of God in the certainty of His promises! The Bible promises are "exceeding great and precious" (2 Peter 1:4) in their certainty. Children, you may take those promises and ask God to fulfill them for you, too. You may say to God, "Thou hast promised to answer sinners when they pray to Thee, Lord. Answer me in grace, and make me Thy child." God is willing to save. Ask Him to give you faith, so that you will love Him and trust Him like Nancy did.

"Grace and peace be multiplied unto you through the knowledge of God, and of Jesus our Lord, according as his divine power hath given unto us all things that pertain unto life and godliness, through the knowledge of him that hath called us to glory and virtue: whereby are given unto us exceeding great and precious promises: that by these ye might be partakers of the divine nature, having escaped the corruption that is in the world through lust" (2 Peter 1:2-4).

Question: What has God promised to sinners? What are God's promises described as in 2 Peter?
Scripture Reading: Hebrews 11.

12. The Bible in the Suitcase

A group of young people were visiting their minister and his wife one evening. The conversation was about praying in front of strangers.

"What do you think of this?" asked a young woman. "Let's say, there are two men on a business trip. They share a hotel room and one of them kneels at his bed to pray before going to sleep. Don't you think that it looks like he's trying to be holy?"

"Not at all," answered a young man, "as long as it's done sincerely. It's your duty to pray wherever you are and in whatever circumstances."

"My husband can tell a story that fits in very well with this," suggested the pastor's wife. "It shows clearly that we may never neglect prayer."

"Yes, it's quite a remarkable story," answered the minister.

"Almost forty years ago now, I went to Boston to be a salesman in a department store. I was only eighteen at the time. I lived in a boarding house in a dormitory room which I shared with some other boys about my own age. On Sunday morning we got up at eight o'clock and as church started at eleven, we had three hours to spare. My mother had packed a brand new Bible in my suitcase, and I wanted to read it. I'd been brought up to read the Bible every Sunday morning. My roommates were reading magazines, and I didn't dare look overly religious.

"I picked up a magazine and tried to read it, but my conscience bothered me so much that I put it down and went to my suitcase. I started to lift the lid of the old trunk, but then I thought I would look like a Pharisee, so I changed my mind and went over to the window. I stood there for about twenty minutes, feeling miserable. I knew I was doing the wrong thing.

"I went back to my suitcase the second time. I had my hand on my Bible, but I was afraid that the other boys would laugh at me, and again I closed my suitcase.

"As I walked again to the window, one of my roommates laughed and said, 'What's the matter with you? You're so restless!

"I laughed too, and then I told them the truth. 'At home I always read the Bible Sunday mornings, but I was afraid that you'd laugh at me.'

"To my surprise, they admitted they both had Bibles in their suitcases, and they had also been wishing to read them, but like me, they were afraid of being laughed at.

"So I said, 'Let's read our Bibles every Sunday morning'.

"The boys agreed and the next moment all three Bibles were out. I tell you, we all felt better after that!

"The following Sunday morning, two boys from another room came in while we were reading our Bibles. When they saw what we were doing, they stared at us, and then exclaimed, 'What's all this? A church meeting?'

"I told them what had happened the week before, and that we had agreed to read a few chapters every Sunday morning before church.

"'Not a bad idea,' remarked one of the visitors. 'You've got more courage than I have. My mom gave me a Bible, too, but I haven't looked in it since I came to Boston. But I guess I should read it, too.'

"The other boys asked one of us to read aloud, and they sat quietly and listened until it was time for church.

"That evening, we three roommates agreed to take turns reading a chapter aloud every evening at nine o'clock. A few evenings after our decision, four or five other boys happened to be in our room talking when the clock struck nine. One of my roommates glanced at me and reached for his Bible. The boys stopped talking and looked enquiringly at the boy with the open Bible on his lap. I explained our custom, and they said that they would stay and listen.

"The result was that, without exception, every one of the sixteen boys in the boarding house spent his Sunday mornings reading the Bible, and it proved to have a good effect on all our lives. I'm not sure if all the boys were converted, but three of them besides myself are now ministers of the gospel. Do you see how much influence one person can have by grace? You must never be afraid to do your duty."

Question: If you were away from home with other people, would you be certain to pack your Bible yourself and read it in front of them? Is reading the Bible something you want to do yourself or do you do it just because your parents do? What happens when your parents aren't there? Why is it important to read the Bible especially when you are away from home? Psalm 119:97-105.
Scripture Reading: Acts 16:20-35.

13. The Blessing of Childlike Faith

There once was a gentleman in New York named Mr. Smith, who said he did not believe in God. He never went to church, of course, and never read the Bible. He did not believe that Jesus is God, or that He died and rose again to save sinners. Yet, when he had been a small boy, his mother had taught him from the Bible. She had filled his memory with Bible verses, and had prayed often with and for him.

Mr. Smith was married. His wife was not a Christian either. They had one child, a bright, intelligent little boy named Tommy. The boy's nurse was somewhat religious, though not religious enough to worry Tommy's parents.

One evening Tommy was lying on his bed, waiting to be tucked in for the night. He had not been a good boy that day, and had been scolded and punished by his nurse and his parents.

All was quiet for a while, when suddenly the child burst into tears, which surprised his parents. His father went to him quickly and asked what was the matter.

"I don't want it, Daddy, I don't want my sins in a book!"

"What do you mean?" asked Tommy's father, not wanting to understand.

"Ellen says God writes down all my sins in a big book, and I don't want them there! I wish they could be wiped out!" Then Tommy cried again, and his father felt like crying with him.

Suddenly, Mr. Smith remembered the truths of the Bible, which his mother had so faithfully taught him when he was a child. After a great inward struggle, he now tried to comfort his weeping child with these truths.

"Don't cry, my dear boy," said Mr. Smith. "It is possible to have them all wiped out."

"What?" cried Tommy eagerly. "Tell me how, Daddy!"

"You get on your knees and ask God for Christ's sake to wipe them out; He is able and willing to do it."

He didn't have to speak twice. In an instant Tommy jumped out of bed and kneeled down by the bedside. He folded his little hands and began to pray. Then he looked up at his father and said, "Daddy, won't you please help me pray?"

This was a hard thing to ask. Mr. Smith had never really prayed in his life. But when he saw the great distress of his child, how could he refuse? So the proud father got down on his knees by the side of his dear son, and asked God to wipe away Tommy's sins and his own sins. Then they got up, and Tommy went into bed again.

"Daddy, are you sure they're all wiped out?"

What a question this was for Mr. Smith! But he felt that he had to answer according to the truths taught him by his mother. "Tommy, the Bible says that if you ask from your heart for Jesus' sake to wash away your sins, and if you are really sorry for what you have done, they shall all be wiped out in God's time."

A tender smile passed over the face of the child as he laid his little head on the pillow. But in a moment, Tommy sat up again. "Daddy, with what did God wipe out my sins? With a sponge?"

This was another difficult question for Mr. Smith. He liked to say to his friends that the Bible was just a collection of stories. People didn't need to be saved, he would say; they didn't need the blood of Jesus. But now he felt that the blood of Jesus was necessary.

"No, my child, not with a sponge, but only with the blood of Jesus Christ who died for sinners. The Bible says, 'The blood of Jesus Christ... cleanses from all sin.'" (1 John 1:7) The father then went on to explain in detail how God can forgive sins based on Jesus making satisfaction to the justice of God for them.

Finally Tommy was satisfied and fell asleep. From that moment, Mr. Smith gave up his false beliefs and began to seek the Lord. The work of the Holy Spirit is amazing and wonderful. He used the simple faith He gave to Tommy for Tommy's father, who was in due time led to the very cross he had so long rejected and yet had been compelled to explain to his son.

"Except ye be converted, and become as little children, ye shall not enter into the kingdom of heaven" (Matthew 18:3).

Question: How does God wipe away sins? What does God say we should become like if we are to enter into heaven?
Scripture Reading: Psalm 131.

14. The Contented Pastor

There was once a pastor who had many trials, but no one heard him complain. He was content and cheerful. A friend asked, "What is your secret? How are you so happy?"

"I use my eyes correctly," was his answer.

The friend was puzzled, so the pastor explained, "When I begin a new day, or face a new trial, I look first to heaven, and remember that I am on earth to glorify God. I pray for His grace and Holy Spirit to wash away my sins in the blood of Jesus Christ, and to use me in His service. Then I look on the earth, and think what a small space I shall need in it when I am dead and buried. Then I look around me, and think how many people there are who have more cause to be unhappy than I have. I think of Hebrews 13:5 and 6: 'Be content with such things as ye have: for He hath said, I will never leave thee, nor forsake thee. So that we may boldly say, The Lord is my helper, and I will not fear what man shall do unto me'."

Question: Are you happy and content?
Scripture Readings: 1 Timothy 6:6; Philippians 2:14; Proverbs 15:16.

15. The Dead Raven

A poor weaver lived in the town of Wuppertal in Germany. Never had anyone heard this man complain. In the midst of all his cares and troubles he would often say, "Well, the Lord helps!"

At this time there was not much work to do. His boss told him that when he had finished making his piece of cloth, there would be no more work for at least six months.

The man was very sad to hear this. "Six months!" he thought. "That's a half year!" When he told his wife, she burst into tears. "How can we get food and clothes for the children if we have no money?" she cried.

All the man could say was, "Well, the Lord helps!" Then he went outside. He watched some boys playing in the street. They were poking at a dead raven with a stick. "The poor bird," thought the man. "I wonder how it died."

When the boys had gone, he walked over to the dead bird. He looked down its throat and saw something shiny. With his pocket knife he pulled it out: a beautiful gold necklace! Quickly, he went to the village jewelry store.

"Do you know whose necklace this might

be?" the weaver asked the jeweler.

"Oh, I know whose it is! that's Mrs. Schelling's necklace."

Mrs. Schelling! She was his boss' wife! The weaver hurried to return the necklace.

When the Schellings heard the weaver's remarkable story, Mr. Shelling said, "I will never put such an honest man out of work. This is your reward: tomorrow you may return to work. I can always use an honest man."

How thankful this poor, yet rich, weaver was! The Lord had helped him once again.

Question: How did this man follow God's eighth and ninth commandments? Can you think of a person in the Bible who was helped by ravens? (1 Kings 17:1-7)
Scripture Reading: Daniel 1:1-21.

16. The Party

Melanie was excited. Her parents were letting her go to a party! She hadn't told them all the details, but she told herself that didn't matter. The plan was to meet at her friend Sharon's house and then go for a sleigh ride. It sounded like fun. At first, her mother had hesitated. But what was wrong with a sleigh ride? Melanie did not tell her mother where they were planning to go afterward.

Melanie's conscience bothered her. She had been raised in a loving, Christian home. Her parents were God-fearing people, and had spoken to their children often about the necessity of being prepared for eternity. Melanie had sometimes felt she had been a very naughty girl. Sometimes she felt impressed by the goodness of God. But these impressions faded over time.

Since this was the first time her parents were letting her go out with friends, Melanie did not want to listen to her conscience. After the evening meal, her father prayed for Melanie's protection. He also asked God to keep her from evil and to save her soul. Melanie almost changed her mind about going to the party. She felt so uneasy.

Instead of enjoying her evening, she was miserable. Sharon was filled with excitement, and didn't notice that Melanie was quiet. The evening was cold and clear, and the snow sparkled in the moonlight. It should have been an enjoyable ride, but Melanie knew where they were headed.

When they reached the bar in the neighboring town, the young people eagerly went inside. Melanie followed silently. She had never been in a bar before. It was dim and smoky. People were dancing. Suddenly, she wanted to go home. She hated this place! Why hadn't she listened to her conscience? She wanted to leave, but she couldn't wait outside. It was simply too cold. Miserably, she waited in a corner of the room. With dismay she noticed that most of the young people in her group of friends were getting drunk. She wanted to pray, but felt so ashamed of herself that she didn't dare.

At last it was time to go. Sharon was drunk too, and Melanie couldn't wait to get home. But what would her parents say? She hadn't known about the dancing, but she had known they were going to a bar.

Melanie didn't sleep much that night. At breakfast the next morning, her mother asked her, "How was the sleigh ride, dear?"

Melanie burst into tears. "It was awful! It was the worst evening I ever had!"

She felt herself to be a great sinner. She had not obeyed the loving warnings of her parents. She had ignored her conscience. She had disobeyed and offended God who had given her so many blessings. How careless, sinful, guilty, and ungrateful she was! Melanie felt she did not deserve forgiveness. Why should God spare such a sinner?

Her parents prayed for and with her. They read many of God's precious promises to her from God's own Word. Finally, Melanie was led to embrace the Savior by faith, and to believe that "the blood of Jesus Christ his Son cleanseth us from all sin" (1 John 1:7). She learned that "the LORD your God is gracious and merciful, and will not turn his face from you, if ye return unto him" (2 Chronicles 30:9).

Question: What should you do when you feel tempted to disobey God and your parents? What commandment did Melanie break when she disobeyed her parents? In Colossians 3:20, who do we please when we obey this commandment?
Scripture Readings: 1 Corinthians 10:13; Hebrews 2:18; James 1:3; Matthew 26:41.

17. The Damage of Gossip

A young man once told many people a mean thing about another person. Later it was found out that the gossip was not true. The young man apologized to the older man whom he had wronged, and asked him if there were anything he could do to make up for his wrong behavior.

The old man grabbed a feather pillow under his arm and took the young man to the top of the church tower. The wind tugged at their hair and flapped their long coats about their legs as they looked at the village and the fields far below them.

The old man handed the young man the pillow. "Rip it open," he said.

The young man was surprised by the strange request. But he did as he was told. Instantly the wind took the feathers, tossing them every which way. A cloud of feathers whirled about their heads, then spread far and wide as thousands of feathers began falling beyond the village, settling on sidewalks, in hedges, in streams, in trees, and in the grass.

"Now," said the old man, "Collect all the feathers and put them back in the pillow."

"All of them?"
"All of them!"
"But that's impossible!"

Placing his hand on the young man's shoulder, the old man said kindly, "I know. I just wanted you to realize how impossible it is to take back gossip."

"A talebearer revealeth secrets: but he that is of a faithful spirit concealeth the matter" (Proverbs 11:13).

Question: What part of the body does James warn us about in James 3?
Scripture Reading: 1 Corinthians 12:19-24.

18. "Thou God Seest Me"

Mr. Williams loved gardening. In his garden grew a special pear tree, of a rare variety. Mr. Williams took very good care of this tree. In the second year, it blossomed, but it bore only one pear. Since there would be no other pears on this special tree that year, Mr. Williams was very anxious about it. He hoped that no rough wind would blow it off. He checked it every morning and every evening, and was glad to find it safe.

Mr. Williams told his children not to touch the pear at all, for the fruit was tender and must not be handled. The thought never occurred to him that one of his children would wish to steal it.

Luke was the youngest son of Mr. and Mrs. Williams. He often looked at that pear, too, and he wished to taste it. Luke should have asked God to cleanse his heart, and to take away the sinful, selfish desire to have that pear. But he did not. He just could not stop thinking about how good that pear would taste.

One night, after everyone was in bed, the thought of that pear kept Luke wide awake. He crept out of bed and went to the window. He opened the window and looked out at the pear tree. He mouth watered as he thought of that delicious pear.

Quickly he pulled on his clothes and crept down the back stairs on his bare feet. Soon he reached the tree. Luke was standing there, looking up at the pear, when he thought, "What will my father say?"

Luke answered the question by telling himself that his father wouldn't know who took it. He made up his mind to pick the fruit and eat it. He reached up to take the pear, but as he moved aside some of the leaves, he noticed a star shining brightly in the dark, clear sky. All at once, these words came to his mind, "Thou God seest me!"

Luke pulled his hands back as though they had been burned, and ran as fast as he could back up the stairs and into bed. He lay there trembling. God had seen him! He was a thief, really, even if he did not actually take the pear.

He cried softly into his pillow and asked God to forgive him, thanking Him at the same time for keeping him from taking the pear. Then he fell asleep and slept soundly.

The next morning, Mr. Williams came in from the garden and said, "The pear is ripe. It's time to pick it, but who is to have it?"

Without thinking, Luke cried out, "God ought to have it!"

Mr. and Mrs. Williams and the other children were surprised at this strange answer. "Why did you say that?" asked Luke's father.

Luke felt his cheeks grow red, and tears came to his eyes. He began to sob. Then he told them that he had almost become a thief the night before. Actually, he was a thief because he had planned to steal the pear. He told them about the star God had used to stop him. Everyone was moved by Luke's confession, but no one was angry with him, for his repentance was real. Gently hugging Luke, his father said, "Then it shall be just as you said: God shall have the pear, and we will give it to Him by giving it to one of His dear children."

"What about our neighbor, Annie?" asked Luke's sister Louise. "She has been sick for so long! Her lips are so often very dry and chapped, and they seldom have any good food to eat. I'm sure she would love a nice, juicy pear!"

So it was decided. Mrs. Williams and Luke went to bring Annie the pear. How she enjoyed it! How thankful she was! It gave Luke more happiness to see Annie's smile than if he had eaten that pear himself. What an important lesson Luke learned! Have you learned it? "Thou God seest me."

Question: When you think about God seeing you at all times, how does this make you feel?
Scripture Reading: Genesis 16:13; Luke 8: 16-18.

19. Unceasing Prayer

Several ministers had gathered to discuss difficult questions, and it was asked how the command to "pray without ceasing" (1 Thessalonians 5:17) could be obeyed. Various suggestions were offered, and at last one of the ministers was appointed to write an essay on the subject for the next meeting. A young maidservant, who was serving in the room, heard the discussion and exclaimed: "What! A whole month to tell the meaning of this text? Why, it's one of the easiest and best verses in the Bible."

"Well, well, Mary," said an old minister. "What do you know about it? Can you pray all the time?"

"Oh, yes, sir!"

"Really? How is that possible when you have so many things to do?"

"Why, sir, the more I have to do, the more I pray."

"Indeed! Well, Mary, how do you do it? Most people wouldn't agree with you."

"Well, sir," said the girl, "when I first open my eyes in the morning, I pray, 'Lord, open the eyes of my understanding,' and while I am dressing, I pray that I may be clothed with the robe of righteousness. While I am washing, I ask to have my sins washed away. As I begin

71

work, I pray that I may receive strength for all the work of the day. While I kindle the fire, I pray that revival may be kindled in me. While preparing and eating breakfast, I ask to be fed with the Bread of Life and the pure milk of the Word. As I sweep the house, I pray that my heart may be swept clean of all its impurities. As I am busy with the little children, I look up to God and pray that I may always have the trusting love of a little child, and as I...."

"Enough, enough!" cried the minister. "These truths are often hid from the wise and prudent and revealed unto babes, as the Lord Himself said. Go on, Mary," he continued, "pray without ceasing. As for us brothers, let us thank the Lord for this lesson."

Question: Can you think of other times during your day when you can pray in the same way as the maid?
Scripture Reading: Luke 11:5-10.

20. A Little Girl and Her Bible

In a crowded train travelling from Boston to Springfield, sat a mother with her little girl. The girl was about eight years old. She had learned early to put her trust in Jesus Christ and to serve the blessed Savior. She had in her hand a Bible, which had been recently given to her as a gift. She was very happy with her new Bible, and treasured it.

Not far from them were sitting a group of young men, who had just been recruited for the United States army. They were talking loudly and swearing dreadfully. One of them in particular, who seemed to be their leader, swore worse than all the rest.

The mother of the little girl was greatly distressed by these horrible oaths. She looked around to see if they could get a seat in another part of the train car, but every seat was occupied. She didn't know what to do.

But the little girl whispered to her mother, "Let me go and give them my Bible, Mama."

The dear girl stepped timidly from her seat and went to the young man who had been the loudest swearer, and presented the Bible to him. She was a little, delicate-looking creature, and as she laid the Book in his hands, she did not say a word, but looked into his face in an earnest way which seemed to say, "Please, don't swear any more!" And then she went back to her own seat.

The effect this little girl's actions had on these young men was amazing. They quietened down at once. Their loud talking stopped. They stopped swearing. Not another oath was heard for the rest of the journey.

The young man who had received the Bible seemed particularly touched. The first time the train stopped, he got out and bought a candy bar. He came and gave it to the girl. Then he stooped down, kissed her cheek, and said, "I thank you, dear child, for your Bible. I will always keep it, and I will read it every day. And when I do, I will always think of you. Will you pray for me too? I will write my parents, and tell them about you. They will tell me you are an answer to prayer."

The little girl never saw the young man again, but she did pray for him often. And she believed the Lord would answer her prayers as well as those of the young man and his parents.

Question: What effect does the Bible have on you? How does it stop you from sinning? Does it help you obey God? (2 Timothy 3:16)
Scripture Reading: John 20:30-31.

21. All In One

A man was once packing his suitcase, preparing for a trip. A friend was watching him. The man said, "Well, I have a little corner left in my suitcase. In it, I am going to pack a map, a lamp, a mirror, a telescope, a book of poems, some biographies, a bundle of letters, a psalm book, and a sharp sword – all in a space of about five by three inches!"

"How are you going to do that?" asked the friend.

"Very easily," replied the man, "for my Bible is all of these things!"

Question: Do you value your Bible as this man did his? Is your Bible your map, light, mirror, and sword? What is meant by these four terms? Look up Ezra 7:10. What did Ezra do with God's Word?

Scripture Reading: Psalm 119:105-112.

22. God's Word is Powerful

A Bible reader visited a prison in London one day. A Bible reader was someone who would visit needy people to read God's Word to them. On meeting the jail keeper, he said to him, "Sir, have you a room in this prison where you keep the worst kinds of prisoners?"

"We certainly do," answered the jail keeper. "They are a miserable bunch of men — mean and badly behaved."

"Will you allow me, sir, to go in there? I wish to try to do them some good," said the Bible reader.

"Impossible!" exclaimed the jail keeper. "It is dangerous to go among those men alone. I should be afraid to let you do that! I never go in myself without being armed."

"Oh! If that is all," answered the Bible reader, "then I am not afraid. I am 'armed.' Please let me go in."

The jail keeper reluctantly agreed to let him enter and gave him a private signal to use if he should get into danger. Then the Bible reader was allowed to enter the cell, and the door was locked behind him.

Finding himself in the cell with several rough-looking men, the Bible reader drew his "weapon" out of his pocket. It was the sword of the Spirit, which is the Word of God. With the Bible in his hand he sat down on the nearest bench, opened the Bible, and read aloud for about fifteen minutes without adding a word of his own. The portions he selected were mostly those which contained the invitations and promises of the Bible. The prisoners listened in silence. When he had finished reading, he asked them, "Would you like me to come tomorrow and read to you again?"

They said they would like that very much. So the next day he came, and the next, until he had been there twelve times. When he arrived on the thirteenth day, the jailor told him, "You may as well have saved yourself the trouble. There is no one left in that cell. They behaved so well that they were allowed to go to a better part of the prison. We keep this cell for the worst ones."

This was good news for the Bible reader. Here was a cell full of men with bad tempers and evil ways, led to behave themselves better through the reading of God's Word. Of course, the Bible reader wished to see changed hearts as well as behavior, but he was encouraged to keep working because he saw that God's Word is powerful.

Question: How could someone who behaves well not be a true Christian? John 3:3; Ephesians 2:8
Scripture Reading: Psalm 146:4.

23. Hidden Treasure

A wealthy man was showing an old college professor through his very expensive home.

The professor was very interested in the man's large library. It was filled from floor to ceiling with expensive books. The professor wanted to stay in this room. But the man moved him back out and carelessly said, "I haven't read one of them, but they sure look good, don't they?"

The professor was shocked. "Why," he answered, "you have a treasure house in this room! But you have neglected it."

When the professor returned home, a thought suddenly struck him. Picking up his beautifully-bound Bible, he shook his head. "Who am I to talk?" he said. "I am guilty of the same thing. Here is my 'treasure house' and how often do I read it?"

Question: What did the professor mean when he said, "I am guilty of the same thing?" Having a beautiful Bible in our house is nice, but what is more important?
Scripture Reading: Amos 8:11-14.

24. How God Used a Thunderstorm

It was some years ago when Mr. Morris, a deacon, travelled through Vermont. As he rode through the mountains, he noticed the darkening sky and the distant rumble of thunder. The path along which he guided his horse led him through a thick forest. He did not think anyone would be living in this part of the woods, so he urged his horse on as fast as he dared. He hoped he would reach a house before the storm came.

Just as the first drops of rain fell, he saw a little house through the trees. It was raining heavily by the time he had tied his horse to the fence post. Without thinking, he dashed into the house without stopping to knock, frightening a woman who was playing with her small son.

"Oh, I'm sorry, Ma'am!" Mr. Morris exclaimed. "I didn't mean to scare you. It's pouring outside, and I wanted to get out of the rain. Do you mind if I wait here until the storm is over?"

"That would be fine," the woman answered. "To tell you the truth, I'm always a little afraid in a thunderstorm, and I'm glad to have someone to keep me company. Let me get you a hot drink," she offered. Soon she was back with some coffee.

"But why are you afraid of thunderstorms?" asked Mr. Morris. "Thunder is the voice of God. He will not harm those who love Him."

The young woman blushed and bit her lip. She had never met anyone who talked like this. Mr. Morris seemed not to notice and asked, "Are any of your neighbours religious?"

"I don't know. My closest neighbors are two miles away. A minister visits them every two or three weeks. My husband went once to see him, but I've never been."

"Do you read the Bible?" questioned the deacon.

"No," the woman shook her head. She wished he wouldn't ask so many questions.

"Why not? Aren't you interested?" he probed.

"I don't really know, sir. You see, I've never read the Bible. I never even went to school because mother died when I was seven and I had to take care of my three brothers. When I got married, my husband taught me to read and write, but we don't have any books to read."

Mr. Morris was shocked, but he did not show it. This woman needed a Bible, but he did not have one with him, nor did he have much money with him.

The storm soon passed and the sun came out.

"I'll be on my way now, ma'am. Thank you very much for allowing me to stay." Mr. Morris paused thoughtfully. He had just enough money to make it home. He had to buy his meals and sleep in an inn two nights. If he gave this woman his money, where would he sleep? He had a loaf of bread with him, so he probably could do without food until he got home. He untied his horse from the fence post and turned to mount. But he felt he could not leave this woman without the Word of God.

"Ma'am," he called, "would you read the Bible if you had one?"

"Oh yes, I would, sir! I've always wondered what the Bible was all about. But we don't have money for that, sir," she said softly.

"What must I do, Lord?" prayed the deacon silently.

Immediately the Lord spoke these words to Mr. Morris in his heart: "He that hath pity on the poor, lendeth to the Lord; and that which he hath given will He pay unto him again" (Proverbs 19:17), and, "Cast thy bread upon the waters: for thou shalt find it after many days" (Ecclesiastes 11:1).

The deacon knew what he must do. He opened his wallet and took out most of his money. "Here," he said, "buy yourself a Bible, and read it often. Ask God to help you understand it. God bless you, ma'am."

"Thank you, sir! I know just where to get one! You're very kind," she smiled through her tears.

The deacon left and continued down the forest path. At sunset he began to look for an inn, but not even a village was to be found. Finally he stopped at a house and asked if there was an inn in the area. The woman laughed and said he'd have to ride most of the night before he would reach an inn. She invited him to stay for supper and spend the night with them. The next morning the woman refused his money.

So it went at every place the deacon stopped. Not one family would accept any payment from him. Mr. Morris was impressed with the Lord's goodness to him. Two days later, he arrived home safely, the remainder of his money still in his wallet. He decided to give that money to a poor widow in town.

A year and a half later, a stranger stopped for supper at the home of the deacon. He explained that he came from the other side of the mountain near the Connecticut River.

"Oh!" smiled the deacon, "Then you might know the Wilsons and the Cartwrights. They live around there, too."

"Yes, I know them very well."

"Do you know if there are more religious people in that area?" asked Mr. Morris.

"Well, besides the Wilsons and the Cartwrights, there are no others in that particular area. But in a small town about thirty miles from the river, there seems to have been a revival. It started in a very unusual way. The first person converted was a poor woman who lived in a secluded part of the forest. When she was baptized, she told us that a stranger had stopped at her house because of a thunderstorm, and spoke to her very seriously. While she listened, she felt concern for her soul. The man was surprised to hear that she had no Bible and gave her money to buy one. She did so the next day, and it was the means for her conversion. She has no idea who the man was, but she believes that God sent him to her. The neighbors noticed a change in her and they were impressed by the goodness and power of the Lord. They began to read their neglected Bibles, and several of them have been converted since then.

The deacon could not help shedding tears as he listened. Suddenly, he exclaimed, "Oh God, Thou hast paid me again!" His heart overflowed with thankfulness and humility. God had used him to bring this woman and others to true conversion.

Question: How did God "pay" the deacon? Why was he thankful? (Luke 15:7) Who is rejoicing in Zephaniah 3:17?
Scripture Reading: Proverbs 19:17; Ecclesiastes 11:1; Psalm 19.

25. Learning by Heart

Arthur ran up to the car and exclaimed, "Grandpa, guess what?" "What?" Grandpa had barely stepped out of the car, and he was surrounded by Arthur and his brothers.

"I memorized one of your favorite parts of the Bible. I learned it for Sunday school. I can say it by heart!" Arthur was obviously proud of himself.

"Which one is it?" asked his grandfather.

"First John 4," stated Arthur. He expected the old man to ask him to recite it for him. Instead, he said seriously, "I'm glad to hear it, my boy. I hope that the Holy Spirit will write that chapter on your heart. That will make you happy for time and eternity."

Arthur quickly ran off to climb up into the tree fort in the back yard. Grandpa followed more slowly and sat in a chair in the shade of a tree nearer to the house. The boys thought he had gone inside to talk with their mother, and did not know he could hear every word that they said.

"Hey! Who said you could come up here?" It was Arthur's voice. "You're too small. It's only for us big kids."

"I am big!" insisted Andrew.

"Jerry, I thought you said it was only for us two. You said it was a secret hideout," Arthur argued.

"Ha!" laughed Andrew. "It's not very secret!"

"Get down! You're not allowed up here!"

"I'm not going down!"

"Get out!" repeated Arthur.

"I'm telling Mom, Arthur!" threatened Jerry.

Arthur ignored him and tried to shove Andrew toward the door. Immediately, Andrew punched him in the chest. It would have turned into a serious fight, had they not been stopped by Grandpa's voice.

"Arthur, come here."

Arthur became frightened when he heard his grandfather's voice, but he tried not to show it. "You're not coming up here again," he whispered angrily to his little brother. Reluctantly, he climbed down the rope ladder and went to meet his grandfather.

Grandpa placed his hand on Arthur's shoulder and asked him to recite the chapter he had memorized. Arthur looked up in surprise. Perhaps he hadn't heard the argument after all. He took a deep breath and began rattling off the verses, looking at his grandfather for approval.

The old man held up his hand. "Slow down. Always think about what you are saying. Start over."

Arthur spoke more slowly. He noticed Grandpa nodding, and he began to think about what he was saying. When he came to verses seven and eight, he began to understand why his grandfather had asked him to recite the chapter.

"Beloved, let us love one another: for love is of God; and everyone that loveth is born of God, and knoweth God. He that loveth not knoweth not God; for God is love."

Arthur looked at the ground and kicked at the dirt. The last two verses stung his conscience.

"If a man say, I love God, and hateth his brother, he is a liar: for he that loveth not his brother whom he hath seen, how can he love God whom he hath not seen? And this commandment we have from him, that he who loveth God love his brother also."

"My dear boy," said his grandfather, "I hope this shows you the difference between head knowledge and heart knowledge. It is quite easy to learn a chapter about love by heart, but we need the grace of God to learn it in our hearts. Head knowledge is not enough, Arthur. It will not keep us from sinning. You have learned this chapter, but it did not keep you from getting into an argument with your brother. When the Lord begins to work in a person's heart, it shows in his life, just like a fruit tree bears fruit. It is good to memorize texts from the Bible, but above all, ask the Lord to apply it to your heart so that you may live what you learn."

Arthur was impressed by his grandfather's loving admonition. Arthur's grandfather was glad to know later that 1 John 4 became a very personal chapter for Arthur.

Question: Memorizing Bible texts is very good, but what is better?
Scripture Reading: 1 John 3:13-24.

26. Mary Jones and Her Bible

Mary lived in Wales. She had poor parents who were weavers.

In Sunday School, Mary heard lessons from the Bible. God blessed these lessons to her heart, and Mary began to love the Bible. Mary's family was poor, and they could not afford to buy a Bible. Besides, Bibles were hard to find and were very expensive at that time.

Mary began to earn money for her own Bible. She cared for children and mended clothes. She kept chickens and sold eggs. She cleaned houses. She did whatever she could to earn money for her own Bible.

After working for six years, she had finally saved enough money. The nearest place to buy a Bible, however, was twenty-five miles away, but Mary eagerly walked the long distance to Reverend Edwards' home. She had been told that she could buy a Bible from the minister.

The next day, after she told Reverend Edwards why she had come, and asked for a Bible, he replied, "I have none. There are two Bibles in that bookcase, but I have promised them to others. I have no extras."

Reverend Edwards' words fell like stones

on Mary's heart. A black despair seemed to come over her like a cloud. All the years of working, waiting, and hoping seemed to rise like a great wave that would sink and crush her. It had all been of no use! The long weary walk yesterday had been useless! How happy she had been yesterday, so full of hope, but all for nothing! At this last thought her feelings gave way, and she burst into tears. Burying her face in her hands, she sank into a chair, for she shook so much that she could not stand. How could she go back without her Bible?

Realizing at once how much the girl wanted a Bible, Reverend Edwards laid his hand on Mary's head. "My child," he said, "you shall have your Bible. I cannot send you away empty, no matter who else goes without. Calm yourself, my child."

He went to the bookcase and, opening a door, brought a Bible and returned to Mary's side. "Take it, Mary," he said, putting it into her hands.

Mary's eyes, still brimming with tears, looked up at him, the light of hope shining in her face. "Is it really for me?" she whispered.

"It is for you, my child," said Reverend Edwards.

Mary rose, and gave faltering thanks to the pastor. Her one desire now was to return to her parents to show them her new treasure. After a hasty meal with Reverend and Mrs. Edwards, she set out on her walk home.

It was later in the morning than the hour at which she had started the day before, but it was a cool, windy day, and pleasant for walking. Mary passed mile after mile of road as one in a dream. Holding her Bible clasped to her breast, head erect, and a smile on her face, she went on, unconscious of everything around her. She had her Bible, her own Bible, and she was on her way home! Weariness, hunger and thirst did not seem to bother her, for she finally had her Bible.

Question: You can feel the love Mary had for the Bible. Why did Mary love her Bible? Do you read, love, and treasure your Bible? Scripture Reading: 2 Timothy 3:14-17.

27. Perfect

r. Thompson was a lawyer. He had never read the Bible and doubted that it was God's Word.

One day he asked a Christian friend, "What books would you recommend that I read to convince me that the Bible is actually God's Word?"

His friend replied, "Read the Bible itself."

Mr. Thompson thought his question had been misunderstood. "What I meant was, that I want to read some books that will convince me that the Bible is true."

But his friend said, "No, do not turn to other books. Read the Bible itself."

Mr. Thompson then read the Bible through, beginning with Genesis. When his friend came to visit he found him deep in thought. Mr. Thompson told his friend that he had read the Ten Commandments in Exodus. "I have been trying to see if I can add anything to it, but I can't. I have thought about what I could take away from it to make it better, but I can't. It is perfect."

Question: Why did Mr. Thompson not need to read other books to be convinced that the Bible is perfect?

Scripture Reading: Exodus 20; Psalm 9:7-14.

28. Samusili's Book

Samusili was a slave boy. He had been stolen from his home in Africa. Now he had to work on a large cocoa plantation in Angola. He had to get up before it was light and work very hard all day. However, Samusili met some workers who spoke his language. They told him about a new way of life. They met together to worship "Yesu" (Jesus) and to read beautiful stories from a good Book.

Samusili began to learn how to read and write from the Book. The more he learned, the more he loved this Book. Before long, however, the owner of the Book moved to another plantation. How Samusili missed and longed for this special Book! He began to pray every day for such a Book. He prayed first thing when he woke up. He often prayed during the long working hours of the day. He earnestly prayed again at night that the Lord would send him such a Book.

One day he received a delightful surprise. As he was emptying a bag of cocoa beans, a book fell out along with the beans! Samusili snatched it up, and recognized the word "Ovikanda" (Epistles) on the cover. The desired Book had appeared as if by a miracle!

When he had the chance, he took the Book to his room. Now he could read again!

Samusili soon shared his secret with some other God-fearing workers. They were very glad! They, too, wanted to learn to read and write. Late at night, after the foreman's light was out, about one hundred slaves met secretly. The call of the screech owl was their signal to come. They used any old paper they could find to copy texts from the Book and hymns which they knew. Their best time to worship God, read His Word, sing, and study their lessons was the late night hours.

When the plantation manager heard what was going on, he raided the "school." He burned all their pencils, paper and handmade books. Poor Samusili was whipped and bound in chains. When other workers came to see him, he said, "I am bound, but they cannot bind the Word of God." He told them about what God says in the good Book.

Later Samusili was set free. Now the Christians were given more work and harder jobs than the others. They suffered persecutions and whippings. In spite of this, they met in the bush as often as they could to worship God. Finally the cruel manager moved back to his own country. Happily, the new manager stopped the beatings and persecution.

Samusili taught the workers from the Book for many years. He told them to pray for faith in God and for grace to believe in Jesus Christ. The Holy Spirit richly blessed his teaching.

In later years, Samusili was told he could go back to his homeland. However, he said, "Here Christ found me; here I shall stay to teach others about Him."

Does he still have the Ovikanda which fell from the bag of cocoa beans? Samusili says, "The pages wore out from use, but it is still in our hearts by the grace of God!"

Question: What can't you do to God's Word?

Scripture Reading: Galatians 3:21-29.

29. The Best Prescription

Martha's forehead was creased with a deep frown. Her eyes were framed with worry lines. Her life was so full of worries and cares! With a deep sigh she lay her hand over her heart which was fluttering again. Her head was aching again, too. It seemed that the more problems she had in her life, the worse she felt.

For the third year in a row the drought had destroyed their crops. The harvest had been very poor again. How could they begin to pay all their bills? Jake had gone to yet another bank this morning. Would he be able to get a loan this time? If this bank turned him away, he had nowhere else to go. Would they have to lose this farm that they had worked so hard day and night to keep?

With all these worries, Martha had become a very nervous person. Jake always tried to cheer her up. "Just think, dear," he would say, "they always say that troubles come in three's. This is our third bad year, so next year is bound to be better!"

But Martha only became more worried. What if Jake couldn't get the money? What if they would lose their farm? What if.... Martha began to feel faint. Where could she turn for help? At last she decided to make an appointment with her doctor.

During her visit to the doctor, Martha carefully described all the problems she was having with her health. She also told how worried she was about all the problems her family was experiencing. The doctor listened carefully and then asked Martha a number of questions. After a brief examination, he asked, "Martha, do you ever read the Bible?"

'Why, no!" exclaimed a puzzled Martha, "But what does that have to do with how I feel?"

"Everything!" replied the doctor kindly. "My prescription for you is this: Go home and read your Bible for an hour every day. Then come back to see me a month from today."

Before Martha could protest, the doctor ushered her from the room and called for his next patient. Surprised to be treated in this way, Martha felt angry at first. But at least she did not have to buy a lot of expensive medicines. It would cost nothing to read the Bible. And it certainly had been a long time since she had looked at the well-worn Book that she had received from her mother before she passed away. Now her conscience accused her. She thought back to how she had become so busy with the children and all the cares of daily life that she had gradually stopped reading her Bible and praying as her work increased.

Martha hurried home. Searching until she found her Bible, she placed it on the table near her favorite chair. Each morning Martha got up half an hour earlier than usual and read the Bible. Then, following the noon meal, she tried to find time to read for a while, and again after the children were in bed at night. The Lord blessed her reading, giving her a sense of His care and protection.

After doing this for a month, she returned to visit the doctor as she had promised. "Well," the doctor said smiling as he looked at her face, "I see that you have followed my prescription faithfully. How do you feel? Do you think that you still need medication?"

"No, doctor," Martha replied, "I feel like a different person now. But how did you know that this was what I needed?"

The old doctor turned to his desk and picked up his open Bible. It was worn and marked, and showed that it had had much use. "Martha," he said earnestly, "reading the Bible is my greatest source of strength and skill. I never go to perform an operation without first reading my Bible. Whenever I have a difficult case, I find help from reading its pages. When I saw how nervous and distressed you were last month, I realized that you did not need any medicine that I could give you. But you needed a source of peace and strength outside of yourself. Therefore I gave you the prescription that I use for myself, for I knew it would work. God blesses the reading of His Word."

"Thank you, doctor," Martha said slowly. "I must admit that I almost didn't follow your advice, but your words made my conscience speak. It had been years since I read my Bible or prayed. How comforting it was to read that not even a sparrow falls to the ground without the will of the Lord! I believe that the Lord is also teaching me that I must look to Him for all my needs, not only for the outward ones, but also for the needs of my lost soul."

"Would you believe," replied the doctor, "that very few of my patients are willing to try this prescription. But I know that if many of my difficult cases turned to their Bibles, they would find the comfort and encouragement that you have found." Finding the place in his Bible, the doctor continued, "God's own Word tells us this in Psalm 19:7-11: 'The law of the LORD is perfect, converting the soul: the testimony of the LORD is sure, making wise the simple.

"The statutes of the LORD are right, rejoicing the heart: the commandment of the LORD is pure, enlightening the eyes.

"The fear of the LORD is clean, enduring for ever: the judgments of the LORD are true and righteous altogether.

"More to be desired are they than gold, yea, than much fine gold: sweeter also than honey and the honeycomb.

"Moreover by them is Thy servant warned: and in keeping of them there is great reward.'

"One of my patients once used the excuse that he stopped reading the Bible because it was too deep for him. He said he could never memorize or remember what he had read anyway. But I told him that it's like putting a woven basket under water. No matter how deep the water, when the basket is lifted out, it immediately empties. Yet as the water runs out, it cleanses the basket. So it is with 'the washing of water by the Word' as we read in Ephesians 5:26."

The doctor in this story has passed away, but his prescription lives on. What a blessing it would be if we, by God's grace, would look to the heavenly Physician who knows what we need before we ask.

Question: What healed Martha's worries? What does the Word of God do to the soul? Scripture Reading: Psalm 12.

30. The Boy and The Bible

Charlie went to school where he learned to love the Bible. One day his mother sent him to the store to buy some soap.

They did not have paper bags or boxes in those days. Instead, the clerks wrapped what you bought in all sorts of paper. Therefore, when Charlie put his soap on the counter, the clerk tore a page from a large book for wrapping paper. But when Charlie saw the wrapping, he exclaimed, "Why, madam! That is a Bible!"

The woman carelessly answered, "Well, what if it is?"

"But it is a Bible," Charlie repeated, "and what are you doing with it?"

"Wrapping soap," she replied.

"But, madam," he cried, "you should not tear up that book or use it like that. It is a Bible!"

"What difference does it make?" she asked. "I bought it for waste paper to use in the store."

"What – the Bible? Oh, I wish it were mine; I would not tear it up like that."

"Well," said the woman, "if you will pay me what I gave for it, you may have it."

"Thank you, madam," he replied. "I will go home and ask my mother for some money."

When he arrived home, he said, "Mother, Mother! Please give me some money!"

"What for?" asked his mother.

"To buy a Bible. The clerk at the store was tearing up a Bible, and I told her that it must not be torn up."

But his mother said, "My dear boy, I cannot give you the money for I have none."

Charlie cried, but there was no money to be had. Still sobbing, he went back to the clerk and said, "My mother is poor and cannot give me money; but please do not tear up the Bible. My teachers told me that it is the Word of God!"

The woman saw that Charlie was greatly concerned. She said, "Well, don't cry. If you will bring me its weight in waste paper, you shall have the Bible." At this unexpected good news, Charlie dried his tears and hurried away. "I certainly will, madam. Thank you!"

Soon he was home again. He asked his mother for some paper. She gave him all she had. Then he went to all the houses in the neighbourhood, asking for paper. When he had collected enough, he hurried back to the store. "Now, madam," he said, "I have the paper!"

"Very well," said the woman, "Let me weigh it."

The paper was put on one side of the scale, and the Bible on the other. The scale showed he had enough. With tears of joy sparkling in his eyes, he cried out, "The Bible is mine!" As he took it from the woman, he exclaimed, "I have it! I have it!" Away he ran to his mother. As he went, he cried, "I have the Bible! I have the Bible!"

Boys and girls, you have also been taught that the Bible is the Word of God. May you also learn to know its value and prize it highly.

Question: Who is the author of the Bible? The Bible is a valuable book because it is the truth of God. What special thing about God's truth is told us in 2 John 2?
Scripture Reading: Psalm 119:46-56.

31. The Old Shoemaker

Several hundred years ago in London, England, a Bible Society was established. The people who started this Bible Society were eager to distribute Bibles, not only in England, but in other countries as well. Nowadays, Bibles are easy to get, and are not very expensive, but long ago it was very hard to get a Bible, because people could not afford one and there were not many Bibles available. So the Bible Society set up little shops, usually in the homes of pastors, where the people in that area could buy Bibles.

But in some countries the Bible was not welcome. France was one of these countries. Most people in France, even today, are Roman Catholic. Finally, the Bible Society found a Protestant pastor living in Nantes who was happy to join the Bible Society and help with selling Bibles.

There was a wandering beggar who lived in the area around Nantes. He tried to earn some money by selling things. One of the few items this beggar owned was a Bible. He soon discovered that people were very interested in this forbidden Book. He found that people did not know what the Bible was about, and used this to his advantage. When he would come to a village he would ask people if he could read to them from the Bible in exchange for money or food.

One day this wandering beggar knocked on the door of a poor shoemaker, begging for money.

"Why are you asking me for money?" asked the shoemaker gruffly. "I need money just as much as you do."

"Well," answered the beggar, trying another tactic, "if you give me a penny, I will read you a chapter of this Bible."

"What's a Bible?" asked the shoemaker. "I never heard of that before."

The beggar was not surprised at this answer — he'd heard it many times before. "It's a book that tells you all about God."

"Well, that would be a penny well spent, I think." The old shoemaker was interested to hear something from this Book, and paid the beggar a penny. Then he sat down with the beggar on a bench outside his little house. The beggar opened the Bible to the third chapter of the gospel of John and began to read. He was a good reader, and the old man listened with a smile on his face. But after several verses, the shoemaker was filled with amazement. Never had he heard such words before! What richness! What simplicity! The words of the gospel were like fresh rain on dry ground.

The beggar reached the sixteenth verse: "For God so loved the world, that he gave his only begotten Son, that whosoever believeth in him should not perish, but have everlasting life." (John 3:16)

The old man's eyes filled with tears. How could it be that he had lived his whole life, attending the Roman Catholic Church in the village, and never heard these words?

The last verse of John 3 filled him with fear: "He that believeth on the Son hath everlasting life, and he that believeth not the Son shall not see life, but the wrath of God abideth on him." (John 3:36) The beggar stopped.

"No! No! Don't stop now!" cried the old shoemaker. "I need to hear more!"

"Give me another penny, sir, and I'll read another chapter," smiled the beggar. He was happy to have someone so interested. He could make some money this way!

The shoemaker got another penny, and the beggar continued reading. Too soon that chapter ended as well, and the shoemaker begged him to go on reading.

"Another penny, another chapter," replied the beggar. "I only read one chapter for each penny."

A third penny was found, and another chapter was read. The old man drank in every word. He was sad when this chapter came to an end, but he had no more pennies to give. "Just tell me where you got this wonderful Book," said the shoemaker.

"Well, sir, I was in Nantes some time ago, begging for food. I knocked on the door of the Protestant pastor there, and he and his wife gave me a fine meal. When I was leaving, they gave me this Bible, and told me it was the best Book ever written. Perhaps it is, but it's gotten me enough money to live on, and I won't be selling it."

The old shoemaker hardly heard him. Nantes. In Nantes he could get a Bible!

After the beggar left, the old man thought about the words he had heard. The book was gone, but the words remained in his heart. Day and night he thought about the words: "For God so loved the world, that he gave his only begotten Son, that whosoever believeth in him should not perish, but have everlasting life."

One morning, about two weeks after the beggar's visit, the old man got up very early, and went to his son's home on the next street.

"Son, I would like you to take care of my shop for a little while," he told him.

"Certainly, father. But why?"

"I am going to Nantes," announced the old shoemaker.

"To Nantes! But father, that's over seventy miles away! How will you get there?" asked his son in confusion.

"I will walk."

"But you are much too old to be walking all those miles! Why must you go to Nantes?"

"I want to get a Bible. I must go. I need that Book."

So the old man started on his journey, using his walking stick for support. When he arrived in Nantes, he found out where the pastor lived and knocked on the door.

"What can I do for you?" asked the pastor kindly when they were seated in the study.

"I was told that you have a book which tells people all about God."

"You mean a Bible," answered the minister.

"Yes, sir. I would like to have one, please," said the old man.

"Do you have money to pay for one?" asked the pastor.

"Pay? I had not thought of that," confessed the shoemaker. "I cannot pay anything, sir. I am only a poor shoemaker. But you gave one to that beggar."

"Where do you live?" inquired the pastor.

When the old man told the minister where he lived, the minister asked him, "How did you get here?"

"I walked."

"But how will you get home?"

"I'll walk back."

"Do you mean to tell me, sir, that an aged man like you will walk one hundred and forty-eight miles to get a Bible? Does it mean that much to you?" the minister asked in amazement.

"Yes, sir, and I will be very happy if I get one. It will be well worth the long walk."

The pastor was very pleased. "Then, my friend, you shall have a Bible! Now, what kind would you like? How about one with a good large print? Do you read well?"

"Never could read a word in my life, sir,"

answered the old shoemaker.

"What?" exclaimed the pastor. "Why do you want a Bible so much if you can't read?"

The old man's eyes filled with tears. "Oh, kind sir, please give me that precious book! I may not be able to read, but my daughter can, and there are three other people in our village who can read. I will ask them to read the Bible to me. The beggar read only three chapters. I want to hear all of it!"

Touched by the old man's earnestness, the minister gladly gave him the Bible. The shoemaker stroked it lovingly, his heart filled with joy. When he got home, he asked his daughter, and the others in his village who could read, if they would take turns reading to him. This they did, happy to do this simple

favor for the old man.

Although he was old, the shoemaker had a keen mind and a good memory, and made rapid progress in his knowledge of the Scriptures. He memorized many passages, repeating them to himself as he worked in his little shop. Then about six months later, the pastor at Nantes was startled by a loud knock at his door. It was the old shoemaker again.

"My friend!" exclaimed the minister. "What brings you here?"

The shoemaker was very agitated. "Oh sir, I'm all wrong. I'm all wrong."

"Come on inside," said the pastor kindly. "Sit down here and tell me what you mean. Why are you all wrong? Who told you that you were wrong?"

"The book, sir. The Bible tells me."

"What does it say?" prodded the minister.

"It says I am all wrong. Here I am, a poor sinner who has been praying all my life to Mary. But she needed a Savior just as much as I do!"

The minister was surprised at the old man's statement. "But you are a Roman Catholic, sir! How did you come to such a conclusion?"

"It says in the book, sir, that she rejoiced in God her Savior — her Savior — so you see, sir, she needed a Savior as much as I do. People tell me that you Protestants have got a religion just like the Bible. I would like to become one of you."

The minister smiled at the old man. "I am happy to hear this, my friend, but before we admit anyone to be a member of our Protestant church, we must examine him."

"Well then, examine me. I am an old man, past seventy years old. I don't know how long I have to live yet, so the sooner you do this, the better."

The minister smiled again. "I am happy to see that you have made up your mind. Let's have lunch, and then I will call on the men needed for the meeting."

After a few hours, the men had gathered to examine the old shoemaker. They asked him many questions.

"What do you know, my friend, of Jesus Christ?"

The shoemaker answered: "The Word

was made flesh and dwelt among us (and we beheld his glory, the glory as of the only begotten of the Father), full of grace and truth" (John 1:14).

"What do you believe about Christ's death?" asked another man.

"The blood of Jesus Christ His Son cleanseth us from all sin" (1 John 1:7).

"What would you say were the privileges of those who are Christ's followers?"

"There is therefore now no condemnation to them which are in Christ Jesus, who walk not after the flesh, but after the Spirit" (Romans 8:1).

"True; and what is the duty of the believer in Christ?" asked the minister.

"Ye are not your own, for ye are bought with a price: therefore glorify God in your body, and in your spirit, which are God's" (1 Corinthians 6:19-20).

The men nodded their approval. "My friend," said the pastor, "evidently you have been taught of God, and so we want to welcome you among us as a brother."

This made the old man very happy, and he was formally admitted as a member of the French Reformed Church, and received a certificate to certify this.

When they returned to the pastor's house after the meeting, the old man asked the minister, "Could you please wrap this certificate up for me? I don't want it to get damaged on my way home."

"Certainly," replied the pastor. He found

some scrap paper and carefully wrapped the certificate.

Cheerfully, the old man went on his way, and when he reached his home, he told his family and friends what had happened. He showed them his certificate, and even asked them to read what was on the scrap paper which had protected his certificate.

Several months passed, and for the third time the pastor in Nantes opened his door to a loud knock. Again, there stood his old friend the shoemaker.

"What? Have you walked all this way again?"

"Oh yes, sir. I've come for the Bible Society meeting."

The pastor looked confused. "Bible Society meeting?" he echoed.

"Yes, there's to be a meeting tonight." With great care the shoemaker unfolded the piece of scrap paper which had wrapped his document. "Look, sir, it says on this paper."

"Oh," answered the minister. "But this is all a mistake. This paper is fourteen years old! You have the right day and month, but this was for a meeting fourteen years ago. We have not had a meeting since then."

Now it was the old man's turn to look puzzled. "Why would you stop having meetings about spreading the Word of God?"

The minister explained that there had been so much opposition that people had lost courage. The pastor smiled suddenly. "But now that you are here, there is no reason not to have a meeting. We will indeed have a meeting this very evening!"

The minister went to several homes, telling Christian friends that there was to be a Bible Society meeting that evening. He asked them to tell others about the meeting.

At the meeting that evening, it was decided that every year there would be an annual Bible Society meeting. The pastor introduced his friend the shoemaker, who told them how the Bible had changed his life. He urged them to continue selling and giving out Bibles, as it was the best means of winning souls to Jesus. He told them that the Bible is the best way to show people their errors, and to bring people to know Christ as their Savior.

The enthusiasm and zeal of this poor shoemaker influenced everyone at the meeting. The people were encouraged to continue their work, and not give in to the opposition. The following year, and the third year, the shoemaker attended the meetings, always urging the people to do their utmost to circulate the Word of God, but he died before the fourth year and went to live forever with his precious Savior. Then he met, face to face, the Author of the Book he loved so well. "Thy words were found, and I did eat them; and thy word was unto me the joy and rejoicing of mine heart: for I am called by thy name, O LORD God of hosts" (Jeremiah 15:16).

Precious Bible! what a treasure
Does the Word of God afford!
All I want for life or pleasure,
Food and medicine, shield and sword;
Let the world count me poor:
Having this, I need no more!

Food to which the world's a stranger,
Here my hungry soul enjoys;
Of excess there is no danger,
Though it fills, it never cloys.
On a dying Christ I feed —
He is meat and drink indeed!

Shall I envy, then, the miser,
Doting on his golden store?
Sure, I am, or should be, wiser;
I am rich: 'tis he is poor;
Jesus gives me in His Word
Food and medicine, shield and sword.

Question: Why did the shoemaker want a Bible even though he could not read? What is the best means of saving souls for Jesus? Scripture Reading: John 3:16; John 3:36; Luke 1:46-47; Psalm 119:97-104.

32. Two Rich Boys

More than a hundred years ago, there were two boys in London who suddenly lost both their parents. One of the boys was about eleven, and the other thirteen years old. Happily, the parents of these boys had taught their sons from the Word of God. The Bible had become precious to these boys, and they loved the Savior who had bled and died for sinners.

But now they had to decide what to do. The only friend they had in the world was an uncle who lived in Liverpool. They had no money, so they couldn't stay in the home their parents had rented, and they couldn't wait for a reply in the mail from their uncle. So they had to pack up their few belongings and set out to find their uncle.

After walking many weary miles they reached a place called Warrington, which is about twenty miles from Liverpool. With their little bundles in their hands, they went to an inn and asked for a night's shelter. The innkeeper, of course, asked them for some money, but they sadly replied that they had none.

"Perhaps we could sleep in the stable, sir," suggested the older boy.

The innkeeper studied the boys, to see

if they might have anything valuable. They wore no gold, as they were very poor, but the man noticed that the older boy had a Bible in his jacket pocket. "You could sell me your Bible, young man," offered the innkeeper. "I'll give you five shillings for it."

It was a great temptation for the boys. They were very tired and hungry. "No, sir," answered the boy with tears in his eyes, "we'll starve before we'll sell our Bible."

The man was surprised to hear the boy's determination. Not many people would make such a bold statement. The innkeeper decided to test them. "I'll give you six shillings for it."

"No, sir," said the boys together.

"Ten," the man offered.

"No!" cried the boy. "This book has been our support and comfort all the way from London. Often, when we were hungry and tired, we sat down at the side of the road and read our Bible. It was as though the Bible was like food and drink and rest to us, for we were given the strength to go on. And it will be our source of strength until we find our uncle in Liverpool."

The younger boy nodded in agreement with his brother's words.

"But," said the man after a moment, "suppose, when you get to Liverpool, you cannot find your uncle, or he refuses to help you. What will you do then?"

"We will trust God, for in this book," answered the younger boy, pointing to the

Bible his brother held, "it says, 'When my father and my mother forsake me, then the LORD will take me up' (Psalm 27:10)."

The innkeeper was amazed. Never had he heard or seen such confidence in God. For several moments he could not speak. Then he said, "My wife would love to meet you, I'm sure. Come with me."

He led them to the kitchen and introduced the two boys to his wife. After the innkeeper had told her the conversation he had had with the boys, the woman wiped her eyes and then bustled about the kitchen fixing them a fine meal. The boys were then led upstairs and slept soundly till morning.

When it was time to leave, the boys tried to thank the innkeeper and his wife, but they waved off their words. "You've been a blessing to us both, dears," said the innkeeper's wife. "God bless you!"

So the boys continued their journey, their hearts overflowing with thankfulness.

Question:Why did the boys feel like the Bible was food and drink? Why do you think the story is titled "Two Rich Boys"?
Scripture Reading: 1 Peter 1:1-9.

33. Words of Life

Long ago, a minister in Scotland had a church near the sea coast. This part of the country was not thickly populated and the houses were far apart. One day, while taking a long walk to visit some members of his congregation who lived a great distance from the church, he noticed a storm approaching. Since he knew he would be caught in the rain before he reached the next home, he looked around for shelter. Not very far away stood an old barn. Hurrying toward it, the minister felt the first raindrops.

When he entered the old barn, the minister found, to his surprise, a group of men seated on the floor. They were a rough looking group and looked up in alarm as the minister slipped into the barn. The minister did not know any of them, but he greeted them in a friendly manner, and asked, "Is it alright if I wait out the storm here? I'll be on my way as soon as it passes."

The men shrugged and nodded. After a while, one of the men asked, "Sir, are you a minister?"

"Yes, I am."

"One of our friends is up in the loft. He's quite sick and we're worried about him.

Would you go and pray with him?"

The minister smiled. "I'd be glad to."

He climbed a ladder into the loft. There, on a bed of straw, lay the poor sick man, who complained of his many sins and expressed his need for the Savior.

The minister sat down on an old stool by his side. The man was very ill.

"My friend," began the minister, "you and I are strangers. We have never met before, and we will most likely never see each other again until we meet at the judgment seat of

God. Now, if I were to tell you that I had in my pocket a medicine that I was sure would cure you of your sickness and make you well again, would you believe me and take that medicine?"

"Certainly, I would," responded the man eagerly.

"Well, my friend, I have no such medicine to heal the sickness of your body," said the minister, "but I have a medicine that will most surely heal the diseases which sin has brought upon your soul and make you fit to

enter heaven. I will not trouble you with any words of my own. Listen while I tell you what God has said about this in His own blessed book. And while you listen, believe the words that you hear and they will, by God's grace, save your soul."

After they prayed together, the minister began, slowly and clearly, to quote passages of Scripture such as these: "Believe on the Lord Jesus Christ, and thou shalt be saved" (Acts 16:31); "The blood of Jesus Christ ... cleanseth us from all sin" 1 John 1:7); "He is able also to save them to the uttermost that come unto God by him" (Hebrews 7:25); "Come unto me, all ye that labor and are heavy laden, and I will give you rest" (Matthew 11:28); "Him that cometh unto me I will in no wise cast out" (John 6:37); "For God so loved the world, that he gave his only begotten Son, that whosoever believeth in him should not perish, but have everlasting life" (John 3:16).

While the minister was repeating these precious words of God, he saw a great change pass over the face of the sick man. The look of sorrow and despair passed away, and a look of calm, quiet peace, hope, and joy took its place. Raising himself on his straw bed, he exclaimed, "I believe it! He has washed away my sin!"

Surely, the blessed Savior can heal poor, sin-sick sinners with His almighty power. David said, "He sent his word, and healed them" (Psalm 107:20). He is the great Physician of souls. Ask Him to cure your disease of sin and to make you clean and pure in His holy sight. God loves to heal all those who come to Him, especially children.

Question: What disease do we all have? Who can cure us from this?
Scripture Reading: John 5:31-47.

Prayer Points

Living for God

1. *Pray that God will help you to be a godly example to others.
    ⌘Ask God to convict you of your sin and show you how you are not living in a virtuous way.

2. *Ask God to give you a gentle spirit and to help you show the love of Christ to the people you meet.
    ⌘Ask God to show you how loving and gentle He is so that you will be humbled and receive Him by grace as your Savior.

3. *Ask the Lord to protect you from sin and temptation. Pray to the Lord for help when you are tempted to disobey His Word.
    ⌘Ask God to show you how wicked sin is and how hurtful it is to Jesus Christ. Ask Him to turn you from your evil ways to follow Him.

4. *Ask the Lord to protect you from hurting others. Pray that He will give you a loving and unselfish heart.
    ⌘Ask God to convict you of your need for salvation. Pray that you will realize once and for all that Jesus is the only way to God.

5. *Thank God for being able to use even our words to draw sinners to Himself. Ask Him to protect you from dishonoring Him with the words that you say.
    ⌘Confess your sin to God for not believing in Him. Ask Him to help you believe.

6.   ✶Ask God to help you love those who hurt you, and to care about their soul.
⌘Confess your sin to God for hurting Him. Ask God to convict you of the sins that separate you from Him. Ask God to give you the gift of faith.

7.   ✶Ask God to help you forgive people who are cruel and nasty to you. Pray that you will always trust God even in bad circumstances.
⌘ Ask God to forgive you for the times you do not care about sin nor ask for His forgiveness.

8.   ✶Thank God for His help day by day. Ask Him to help you to trust Him for all your needs.
⌘ Ask God to show you how much you need His salvation every hour of the day.

9.   ✶Ask God to teach you how to pray to Him.
⌘ Pray to God about your own soul and ask Him to show you how much you need Him and to lead you to beg for His eternal protection.

10.   ✶Thank God for listening to needy sinners like you.
⌘ Ask God to show you that having faith in the Lord Jesus Christ is the only way to be ready for death.

11.   ✶Thank God for His promises. Ask Him to help you tell others about His great faithfulness.
⌘ Ask God to show you through His Word and power how faithful and trustworthy He is.

12.   ★Thank God for giving you the Bible. Ask Him to help you remember it and obey it and to never be ashamed of following God's Word.
⌘ Ask God to give you a love of His Word. Ask Him to use it to convict you of your sin and your need for Christ.

13.   ★Ask God to help you conquer temptation and live your life honoring and working for Him.
⌘ Repent of your sins and ask God to not let you go on living without Him.

14.   ★Ask God to help you to be happy and content. Thank Him for Himself and for the free offer of salvation to sinners.
⌘ Ask God to show you the one thing you need: Himself.

15.   ★Thank God for providing for your daily needs, physically and spiritually.
⌘ Ask God to show you that He is the one thing you need to be happy.

16.   ★Thank God for the godly example of friends and family who love Him.
⌘ Ask God to give you a tender conscience. Ask God to make you listen to it and His Word.

17.   ★Ask God to protect you from saying hurtful and false words. Ask Him to control your tongue so that your words honor Jesus.
⌘ Ask God to convict you of the sin of refusing and ignoring His salvation.

18.   ★Thank God for His ever watchful presence and that there is nothing hidden from Him.
⌘ Repent of living life as though God doesn't

see you. Ask God to convict you of the seriousness of all sin and disobedience to Him.

19. ★ Thank God for being the hearer and answerer of prayer. Thank Him that you can pray by yourself at any time and in any place.
⌘ Ask God to change your heart from one of selfish pride to one of dependence upon Him.

The Value of Scripture

20. ★Pray for people you know who do not know Jesus Christ as their Savior. Ask God to bring them to Himself.
⌘ Ask God to give you a saving knowledge of Himself.

21. ★Ask God to show you how to honor Him today and obey Him.
⌘ Ask God to show you the sin in your heart. Ask for forgiveness and for help to stop sinning in the future.

22. ★Ask God to teach you from His Word and for His Word to change you and make you more like His Son Jesus Christ.
⌘ Ask God to show you who His Son Jesus Christ really is. Ask Him to convict you of sin and of Christ's love for sinners.

23. ★Thank God for giving you His Word to listen to and read for yourself. Ask Him to help you to cherish it.
⌘ Ask God to give you a love and regard for His Word. Pray that He will convict you of its truth and lead you to submit yourself to Him.

24. ✶Pray to God for missionaries who give God's Word to those who have not heard about Him.
⌘ Pray that when you hear about Christ and His love you will not reject Him.

25. ✶Ask God to remind you of His Word throughout the day so that you can obey Him and honor Him.
⌘ Ask God to show you how you are a sinner. Ask Him to take away your desire to sin and give you a heart of love for Himself. Ask Him to bless His word to your heart.

26. ✶Thank the Lord that you have the Bible and so many books based on the Bible. Ask God to give you understanding of His Word as you read it.
⌘ Ask God to use His Word to show you your sin. Ask Him to stop you in your sin and turn you towards Himself. Ask Him to forgive you for not heeding the Bible's warnings.

27. ✶Thank God that you can read the Bible and do not need any other guide.
⌘ Ask God to give you a desire to find out about Him and His Word and to surrender your life to Him.

28. ✶Ask God to protect and encourage your pastor and other people who teach you the truths of God's Word.
⌘ Ask God to give you a desire to listen to His servants and follow Christ, whom they love.

29. ✶Bring your anxieties to God because He cares for you. Confess that you are sorry for doubting His power to take control of the problems in your life. Thank Him for His love.

⌘ Ask God to show you that your soul's safety is the one thing you shouldn't rest for or stop worrying about until you know it's safe with God.

30. ★Thank God for the value of His Word and all that He teaches you through it. Thank Him for teaching you about sin and salvation.
⌘ Ask God to convict you of your sinful disrespect for God's Word. Ask Him to reveal Himself to you as the author of the Bible and its truth.

31. ★Pray for the organizations around the world that give the Scriptures to many people in many languages. Pray that they will always remain faithful to God's Word.
⌘ Pray that you will turn from seeking your own selfish ambitions to seeking after righteousness. Pray that God will change you, that you will no longer look on the Bible as just another book but the living, true Word of God.

32. ★Thank God that His Word lasts forever and that everything God says is both true and trustworthy. Thank Him that His Word contains everything you need to know.
⌘ Repent of your disbelief in God and His Word. Ask Him to show you Himself and give you a personal conviction of His power and who He is. Ask for forgiveness for thinking you can live without Him.

33. ★Pray that you will treasure the salvation of Christ and be humbled by what it cost Him to offer this to you. Thank Him that His Word heals your heart's sicknesses.
⌘ Pray that God through His Word will open your heart to see how badly you need His salvation.

Scripture Index for Book 1

13. Psalm 131
    Matthew 18:3
    1 John 1:7

14. Proverbs 15:16
    Philippians 2:14
    1 Timothy 6:6
    Hebrews 13:5-6

15. 1 Kings 17:1-7
    Daniel 1:1-21

16. 2 Chronicles 30:9
    Matthew 26:41
    Colossians 3:20
    1 Corinthians 10:13
    Hebrews 2:18
    James 1:3
    1 John 1:7

17. Proverbs 11:13
    2 Corinthians 12:19-24
    James 3

18. Genesis 16:13
    Luke 8:16-18

19. Luke 11:5-10
    John 6:35
    1 Thessalonians 5:17
    1 Peter 2:2

20. 2 Timothy 3:16
    John 20:30-31

21. Psalm 119:105-112
    Ezra 7:10

22.   Psalm 146:4
       John 3:3
       Ephesians 2:8

23.   Amos 8:11-14

24.   Psalm 19
       Proverbs 19:17
       Ecclesiastes 11:1
       Zephaniah 3:17
       Luke 15:7

25.   1 John 3:13-24
       1 John 4

26.   2 Timothy 3:14-17

27.   Exodus 20
       Psalm 9:7-14

28.   Galatians 3:21-29

29.   Psalm 12
       Psalm 19:7-11
       Ephesians 5:26

30.   Psalm 119:46-56
       2 John 2

31.   Psalm 119:97-104
       Jeremiah 15:16
       Luke 1:46-47
       John 1:14; 3:16, 36
       Romans 8:1
       1 Corinthains 6:19-20
       1 John 1:7

32.   Psalm 27:10
       1 Peter 1:1-9

33.   Psalm 107:20
       Matthew 11:28
       John 3:16; 5:31-47; 6:37
       Acts 16:31
       Hebrews 7:25
       1 John 1:7

Answers

1. Discuss.

2. Be kind to them. He forgave them.
   We are told to deny ungodliness and worldly lusts. We are told to live soberly, righteously and godly, looking forward to the glorious appearing of the great God and our Savior Jesus Christ. (Titus 2:12&13)

3. Sin and the Devil.
   Sin is destructive and against God. If we guard against temptation with God's help, He will deliver us.

4. They will have long lives.
   It warns us against being influenced by the world and other people and taken away from Christ.

5. Verse 7.

6. Discuss.

7. To those who come to Him confessing their sin.
   Danny and God.

8. Discuss. Yes.

9. Forgiveness.

10. They could defend the country because they asked God for His help.

11. To answer sinners when they pray to Him.
Exceeding great and precious promises.

12. Discuss.

13. With Christ's blood shed for us on the cross.
Little children.

14. Discuss.

15. He did not steal; he did not lie.
Elijah (1 Kings 17:1-7).

16. Discuss (ideas: pray; read God's Word.)
The fifth commandment.
God.

17. The tongue.

18. Discuss (i.e: He sees all our sin even secret sins; He sees all sin even unpunished sin; He sees our obedience too; He knows whether we love Him or not.)

19. Discuss.

20. Discuss. 2 Timothy 3:16 - profitable for doctrine, for reproof, for correction and for instruction in righteousness.

21. Map: It shows us where to go in life - it is God's rule to direct us. Light: It shows us the way to go and how to obey God in a dark and sinful world. Mirror: It shows us ourselves and our sins. Sword: It protects us and defends us against temptation and the devil.
Ezra prepared his heart to seek God's Word, do it and teach it.

22. They must be born again; salvation is the gift of God, not of works.

23. The Bible is God's Word and full of exceeding great and precious promises. Reading and believing the Bible is better and more important than owning one.

24. Christians rejoice, as Christ did, when they hear of sinners who are saved. (Luke 15:7).
God.

25. Applying these texts to our hearts.

26. Discuss.
God blessed the lessons to her heart.

27. He couldn't add anything to it or take anything from it to make it better.

28. You can not bind God's Word.

29. Reading the Bible.
    Converts the soul. Makes wise the simple.

30. God. It shall be with us forever.

31. So that others could read it to him.
    The Word of God.

32. It gave them rest and strength to go on.
    Two rich boys: they were rich because of their great Heavenly Father and His spiritual provision for them in Christ as well as how He provided for their physical needs.

33. Sin.
    The Lord Jesus Christ.

Author Information

Dr. Joel R. Beeke is president and professor of systematic theology and homiletics at Puritan Reformed Theological Seminary, pastor of the Heritage Netherlands Reformed Congregation in Grand Rapids, Michigan, editor of Banner of Sovereign Grace Truth, editorial director of Reformation Heritage Books, president of Inheritance Publishers, and vice-president of the Dutch Reformed Translation Society. He has written or edited fifty books (including several for children), and contributed fifteen hundred articles to Reformed books, journals, periodicals, and encyclopedias. His Ph.D. is in Reformation and Post-Reformation theology from Westminster Theological Seminary. He is frequently called upon to lecture at seminaries and to speak at Reformed conferences around the world. He and his wife Mary have been blessed with three children.

Diana Kleyn is a member of the Heritage Netherlands Reformed Congregation in Grand Rapids, Michigan. She is married to Chris, is the mother of three children, and has a heart for helping children understand and embrace the truths of God's Word. She is the author of *Taking Root and Bearing Fruit*, stories about conversions and godliness written for children. She and Dr. Beeke have recently co-authored Reformation Heroes, which tells the life story of about forty Reformation figures for children ten years and older. She also writes monthly for the children's section in *The Banner of Sovereign Grace Truth*.

Building on the Rock
Books 1-5

If you enjoyed this book:

Book 1
How God Used a Thunderstorm
Living for God and The Value of Scripture

You will also enjoy the others
in this series
by Joel R. Beeke and Diana Kleyn

Book 2
How God Stopped the Pirates
Missionary Tales and Remarkable Conversions

Book 3
How God Used a Snowdrift
Honoring God and Dramatic Deliverances

Book 4
How God Used a Drought and
an Umbrella
Faithful Witnesses and Childhood Faith

Book 5
How God Sent a Dog to Save a Family
God's Care and Childhood Faith

Jorgan's Raccoon

J organ Scheuler lived in a log cabin in the Rocky Mountains. His father and brothers did not care for religion. Ever since his mother died, Jorgan was raised without hearing the Bible read. He grew up learning to fight, drink, and swear. He never thought about those things which are good.

Jorgan's family depended on hunting and fishing for their food. They hunted for deer, wild turkeys and raccoons. One Sunday night, Jorgan went hunting with his three brothers. The moon was full as they entered the forest. Before long, George, his oldest brother, whispered, "Look! There's a big raccoon up in that tall tree."

"But we can never get that one!" answered Ernest quietly, "That raccoon is up way too high." The boys did not have a gun, so someone would have to climb the tree to shake the raccoon down.

"Wait!" Jorgan whispered, "I can climb almost as well as any raccoon. I'll climb that tree. We can't miss a big one like that!"

Jorgan began climbing, with his eye on the branch where the raccoon was hiding. Higher and higher he climbed until at last he was level with the branch. The raccoon began to back up going farther and farther out on the limb. Jorgan carefully climbed onto the branch, giving it a shake. But the raccoon still hung on. Carefully, Jorgan inched his way closer, shaking the branch as he went. But his shaking was not enough to knock the raccoon down. With all his might, Jorgan gave one more hard shake. But in the next instant, the branch broke and he was falling down, down, down.

Terrified, Jorgan cried out, "Lord, have mercy on me!"

As soon as the cry left his lips, Jorgan's hands caught hold of a branch. There he hung, still high in the tree, with no more branches under him. He felt as though he hung between heaven and hell. "If I let go of this branch," he thought, "I will fall straight down into hell!" In vain he struggled to climb back on the branch. Again he cried out, "Lord, have mercy on me!" He received strength to climb back on the limb, and was then able to slowly climb back down the tree. When he reached the ground, he was too weak to stand. George and Ernest helped their shaken brother walk home. They put him to bed.

But Jorgan could not sleep that night. What terrible thoughts filled his mind! "What if the branch I caught had broken? The devil would have me now. I would be burning in hell!" Jorgan tossed and turned all night with terrible thoughts filling his head.

Jorgan went to work the next morning as usual. But he could not laugh and swear as he usually did. What a burden he had to carry! "What's the matter, Jorgan? You look so sad. Are you sick?"

Jorgan thought to himself, "Yes, I am sick. But sin is the cause of it." He did not know what to do. He had never prayed except when he hung helpless in the tree. He had no Bible and he had never heard a minister preach. "I must find a Bible," he thought, "and I must find a minister."

Jorgan remembered that his mother's Bible was hidden in an old trunk. She had died when Jorgan was still a child, and in anger, Jorgan's father had put her Bible away. Now Jorgan sneaked into the cabin and found it. He began to read the Bible every spare minute that he had. But the more he read, the heavier his burden became. He saw hell and punishment in everything he read. He read that the wicked would burn in hell and that there was no peace for the wicked forever. Jorgan knew he was very wicked. He felt that all these curses were on his head. How miserable he became! "If the Bible does not take away my sin, whatever can I do?" he sighed.

Jorgan began to escape to the woods where he would fall down on his knees behind a tree. He tried to pray, but didn't know what to pray. He no longer wanted to be with his brothers and friends. It made him feel terrible to hear them laughing and swearing. He tried to escape by working on the opposite side of the field. Whenever he could, Jorgan would go into the woods to pray. "Jorgan's head is all mixed up," his brothers would say. "It happened when he fell from the tree."

Although Jorgan still tried to read the Bible and pray, he only became more miserable. Every day he read and read, but one day he became so miserable that he thought he would surely die. Yet he knew that he had to continue reading the Bible, even though he only saw hell before his eyes. That day, however, when he began to read, he suddenly read about Jesus. He saw that Jesus could stand between him and his sins. What a joy filled his heart! There was a possibility for salvation in Jesus Christ for a sinner like him.

A new love for Jesus filled Jorgan's heart. He could not wait to share the wonderful news with his brothers. He ran to the field to share his wonderful experience, but his brothers only laughed at him. They had never seen their sins. They did not feel their need for the Lord Jesus. "Jorgan," they replied, "your mind is still mixed up. You don't know what you are talking about."

Years later, Jorgan was working as a blacksmith in a nearby town and he saw Reverend Morris ride past on his horse. Excitedly, Jorgan mounted his own horse and rode after the minister. "Reverend! Please stop. I must speak with you."

Reverend Morris stopped and waited for Jorgan to catch up. Without introducing himself, Jorgan began speaking rapidly. "Oh

Reverend! I have waited for years to speak to a minister of God's Word. I have longed to tell what has happened in my soul. Come to my cabin so I may tell you about it."

When Reverend Morris saw the woods, he hesitated. But when he saw how sincere Jorgan was, he followed him. Soon they reached the rough log cabin that was Jorgan's home. With tears of thankfulness streaming down his face, Jorgan told of the misery and struggles he had experienced, but also of how he had found Jesus in the Bible. He shared his great joy in seeing Jesus stand between God and his sins.

Reverend Morris was impressed by Jorgan's conversion. He saw that Jorgan's only teacher was the Spirit of God who had applied the Bible to his heart. No minister had been necessary for his conversion. He saw that awakened sinners all experience the same thing—misery, deliverance, and thankfulness. Jorgan had felt his burden of sin; he had turned to the Bible for salvation and deliverance, and he had returned to God in thanksgiving. But above all, Jorgan's conversion shows the gracious care of the Great Shepherd, Jesus Christ, for His sheep.

Question: Who was Jorgan's only teacher? In Nahum 1:7, what do we learn about God?
Scripture reading: Psalm 51.

From the fourth book in the series:
How God Used a Drought and an Umbrella - Faithful Witnesses and Childhood Faith.

As Grandfather Does

Jacob and Anna lived with their little boy, John, in the German village of Berheim. John was blessed with a God-fearing grandfather who had prayed for him ever since he was born. When he was baptized, his grandfather had chosen the name "John" for him, saying, "May he be loved by God in time and throughout all eternity."

Grandfather often came to visit little John. Many times he would lay his hand on John's head and say, "The Lord bless you, and keep you as the apple of His eye." Those prayers were not left unanswered.

On Grandfather's sixtieth birthday, John went with his parents to see him. John was very happy to spend the whole day with his grandfather. His father had to go to the farm for the day, but promised to return that evening. A terrible thunderstorm arose, however, which made it impossible for him to return. Therefore, John and his mother had to spend the night at Grandfather's house. John was delighted, but his mother felt uneasy in Grandfather's presence.

When evening came, everyone gathered together. Grandfather opened his large Bible and read a chapter. He then offered up an earnest and childlike prayer out of the fullness of his heart. Everyone then went to bed.

The following morning, Anna left to walk back with her child. It was a lovely summer day, and the walk through the woods was very pleasant. John loved flowers and seldom walked past them without stopping. But today he walked behind his mother as seriously and quietly as though there were not a single flower to be seen. Anna did not feel much like talking either. Her mind was uneasy, but she did not know why.

Suddenly, John stood still, looked up in his mother's face, and asked, "Mother, why doesn't Father do as Grandfather does?"

His mother became somewhat confused. "Why don't you go and look for flowers?" she suggested, and walked on.

So they went on silently, but John was not thinking about flowers. Soon they came to the top of a hill where there was a beautiful view of the distant mountains. Anna sat down to rest for a while, and John sat beside her. "Mother," he said for the second time, "why doesn't Father do as Grandfather does?"

Anna felt impatient. "Well," she answered rather sharply, "What does Grandfather do?"

"He takes the large Bible," said John, "and he reads and prays."

His mother blushed. "You should ask your father about it," she answered.

When they reached home, Father was not there. He had gone to harvest in a field quite far away and would not be back until evening.

John's mother knew this and thought she would put her boy to bed early. She hoped that by morning he would have forgotten his question.

But she was mistaken. As she was going to undress him, he said, "Mother, please let me wait until Father comes home."

At eight o'clock, his father returned. John ran up to him directly and asked, "Father, why don't you do as Grandfather does?"

His father looked surprised. The question was unexpected. "What are you doing up, John?" he asked, "Go to bed now; it's late."

John was silent, but went sorrowfully to bed. He got up the next morning with still more sadness. He was a different child from what he usually was. He sat silent and sad at the breakfast table, with his hands folded and head down. He had not touched his milk. "What is the matter, John? Why don't you eat?" asked his mother.

John was silent.

After a little while she asked again, "What is it, son?" He looked up at his mother very sadly for a moment and bowed his head again. His father and mother had finished, and his mother was clearing the breakfast table. His mother asked a third time, "John, tell me what is bothering you."

Then the boy answered, "I want so much to pray, Mother; but no one will pray with me. I guess I must pray alone."

This was too much for Anna. Tears filled her eyes. She hurried into the next room to tell her husband what the child had said. But he had heard what John had said, for the door was left open. His conscience was touched. "John is right," he said, "and we are wrong." Then they fell on their knees together for the first time in their married life. They prayed a prayer with few words but with many tears. It was the publican's prayer: "God be merciful to us, sinners!"

The happy day had arrived when little John no longer had to pray alone. Father and Mother now began to bend their knees before the Lord to ask for His mercy and forgiveness. They asked for a new heart and for grace for themselves and their child to live entirely for Him.

Do you love to pray as little John did? You must be thankful for, and attentive during, family prayer at home.

Question: In the chapter in Scripture where the publican prays, who else was praying at the same time? Luke 18:9-14. In the following Scriptures, what advice does God have for families: Joel 1:3; Deuteronomy 6:6-7? Scripture reading: 2 Chronicles 7:14; Jeremiah 29:13; Mark 11:24; James 5:16; 1 John 3:22.

From the fifth book in the series:
How God Sent a Dog to Save a Family - God's Care and Childhood Faith.

6. Flying Bread

Wilsie and Waylo sat shivering in their hut. A fierce wind blasted the icy snow down through the smoke hole.

"We may as well admit it," complained Halona, the children's grandmother, "we're going to starve."

The three Indians huddled around the little fire. It burned poorly for the wood was wet. Clouds of smoke stung their eyes.

"I found ten of our sheep dead just now," stated Waylo miserably.

"Ten more?" cried the old woman, "Before this week is over they'll all be dead from cold and hunger. Then there will be nothing left for us to eat." She closed her eyes and began chanting a heathen prayer in her own language.

"Grandma," interrupted Wilsie, "we still have a little bit of flour. I can make two or three loaves of bread. If we eat one slice each per meal, we'll have enough for about four days."

"And then what?" growled Waylo.

"By that time, I think God will have sent help," Wilsie answered cheerfully.

Waylo laughed bitterly. "If I could ride to the white man for help, then maybe God could help us. But now that my pony is dead, I'm stuck here. Grandma's right, Wilsie. If it is the will of the gods that we must die, I am ready."

Grandmother knelt by the fire and fanned the weak flames. It would be hours before the lamb chops would be ready to eat. Waylo tried not to think how good the meat would taste.

Wilsie whisked the snow off an old trunk and took out her Bible. She wanted her grandmother to know the One who could send help from above. Wilsie was sure the Lord would answer her prayer for food. She told the story of Elijah and the ravens. "When Elijah was hungry, God sent ravens with food. Don't you think God will help us if we trust Him?"

"Perhaps, perhaps," said Halona thoughtfully. Wilsie noticed a hopeful look in her eyes.

"I'd like to see that happen," thought Waylo.

The next day was bitterly cold. More sheep died, for they had no shelter from the wind. There they stood, frozen stiff. They had not even toppled over.

"O Lord God, send us help before we die, for Jesus' sake," prayed Wilsie.

"Look!" shouted Waylo, interrupting Wilsie's silent prayers. "Grandma! Wilsie! Come outside! An airplane!"

Sure enough, they could hear the faint hum of an airplane.

Wilsie put on her coat and grabbed her red sweater. "Let's wave to them," she shouted. "Maybe they'll see us!"

The children waved and shouted at the tops of their voices, forgetting that the pilots would not be able to hear them. But the pilots had seen them. The men in the little plane were on the lookout for Indians in just such a need.

Halona watched the small yellow plane swoop low over their hut. With tears in her eyes, she saw strong sacks of flour, beans, sugar, and dried fruit being dropped from the plane. Waylo stared open-mouthed as a side of bacon fell a short distance from where he stood. Wilsie jumped aside to dodge packages of coffee and raisins. Indeed, the heavens were raining food!

Halona was not ashamed of her tears as she gathered the food into the hut. There would be enough for the rest of the winter. "It was the white man's God who sent His raven to us," she said, hugging her grandchildren.

Question: God fulfilled the bodily needs of these three Indians. He can do this for you too, boys and girls, but He can also fulfill your spiritual needs. Do you ask Him for this?
Scripture reading: 1 Kings 17:1-16.

Other books published by Christian Focus Publications in connection with Reformation Heritage Books.

Bible Questions and Answers
by Carine Mackenzie
ISBN 978-1-85792-702-3

Teachers' Manual by Diana Kleyn.
ISBN 978-1-85792-701-6

Doctrines and subjects covered in
these two titles include:

God

Creation

How man sinned

What happened because of sin

Salvation

Jesus as Prophet, Priest, and King

The Ten Commandments

Keeping God's Laws

The way to be saved

Experiencing God's salvation

Baptism and the Lord's Supper

Prayer

Where is Jesus now?

Death

Hell

Heaven

Classic Devotions
by F.L. Mortimer

Use these books alongside an open Bible and you will learn more about characters such as Cain and Abel, Abraham, Moses and Joshua, amongst others. You will enjoy the discussion generated and the time devoted to devotions and getting into God's Word. Investigate the Scriptures and build your knowledge with question and answer sessions with F. L. Mortimer's range of classic material. Written over a hundred years ago, this material has been updated to include activities and discussion starters for today's family.

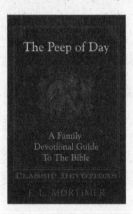

ISBN: 978-1-85792-585-2

Line upon Line Book One
978-1-85792-586-9

Line upon Line Book Two
978-1-85792-591-3

Mary Jones and her Bible

a true life story
a classic favorite

The traditional story of the young Welsh girl who treasured God's Word and struggled for many years to get a copy of her own. An excellent reminder of our Christian heritage.

ISBN: 978-1-85792-568-5

The Complete Classic Range: Worth Collecting

Saved at Sea
ISBN: 978-1-85792-795-5

A Basket of Flowers
ISBN: 978-1-85792-525-8

Christie's Old Organ
ISBN: 978-1-85792-523-4

A Peep Behind the Scenes
ISBN: 978-1-85792-524-1

Little Faith
ISBN: 978-1-85792-567-8

Children's Stories
by D L Moody
ISBN: 978-1-85792-640-8

Mary Jones and Her Bible
ISBN: 978-1-85792-568-5

Children's Stories by J C Ryle
ISBN: 978-1-85792-639-2

Childhood's Years
ISBN: 978-1-85792-713-9

**Fiction books with God's message
of truth:
Freestyle - 12+
Flamingo - 9- 12
Fulmar - 7-10 years
Check out our webpage for further
details: www.christianfocus.com**

Martin's Last Chance
ISBN: 978-1-85792-425-1

A Different Mary
ISBN: 978-0-90673-195-6

Sarah & Paul Make a Scrapbook
ISBN: 978-1-87167-635-8

The Broken Bow
ISBN: 978-1-87167-698-3

The Big Green Tree at No. 11
ISBN: 978-1-85792-731-3

TRAILBLAZERS

Gladys Aylward, No Mountain too High
ISBN 978-1-85792-594-4
Corrie ten Boom, The Watchmaker's Daughter
ISBN 978-1-85792-116-8
Bill Bright, Dare to be Different
ISBN 978-1-85792-945-4
Adoniram Judson, Danger on the Streets of Gold
ISBN 978-1-85792-660-6
Amy Carmichael, Rescuer by Night
ISBN 978-1-85792-946-1
Billy Graham, Just Get Up Out Of Your Seat
ISBN 978-1-84550-095-5
Isobel Kuhn, Lights in Lisuland
ISBN 978-1-85792-610-1
C.S. Lewis, The Storyteller
ISBN 978-1-85792-487-9
Martyn Lloyd-Jones, From Wales to Westminster
ISBN 978-1-85792-349-0
George Müller, The Children's Champion
ISBN 978-1-85792-549-4
Robert Murray McCheyne, Life is an Adventure
ISBN 978-1-85792-947-8
John Newton, A Slave Set Free
ISBN 978-1-85792-834-1
John Paton, A South Sea Island Rescue
ISBN 978-1-85792-852-5
Helen Roseveare, On His Majesty's Service
ISBN 978-1-84550-259-1
Mary Slessor, Servant to the Slave
ISBN 978-1-85792-348-3
Joni Eareckson Tada, Swimming against the Tide
ISBN 978-1-85792-833-4
Hudson Taylor, An Adventure Begins
ISBN 978-1-85792-423-7
William Wilberforce, The Freedom Fighter
ISBN 978-1-85792-371-1
Richard Wurmbrand, A Voice in the Dark
ISBN 978-1- 85792-298-1

Bible Stories and Non Fiction

Bible Time, Bible Wise, Bible Alive and The Bible Explorer

All by Carine Mackenzie.

Paul - Journeys of Adventure
ISBN: 978-1-85792-465-7

Noah - Rescue Plan
ISBN: 978-1-85792-466-4

Joseph - God's Dreamer
ISBN: 978-1-85792-343-8

Esther - The Brave Queen
ISBN: 978-1-84550-195-2

Mary - The Mother of Jesus
ISBN: 978-1-84550-168-6

Gideon - Soldier of God
ISBN: 978-1-84550-196-9

ISBN: 978-1-85792-533-3

BIBLE ALIVE SERIES

Jesus the Storyteller
ISBN: 978-1-85792-750-4

Jesus the Child
ISBN: 978-1-85792-749-4

Jesus the Saviour
ISBN: 978-1-85792-754-2

Jesus the Healer
ISBN: 978-1-85792-751-1

Jesus the Miracle Worker
ISBN: 978-1-85792-752-8

Jesus the Teacher
ISBN: 978-1-85792-753-5

The Adventures Series
An ideal series to collect

Have you ever wanted to visit the rainforest? Have you ever longed to sail down the Amazon river? Would you just love to go on Safari in Africa? Well these books can help you imagine that you are actually there.

Pioneer missionaries retell their amazing adventures and encounters with animals and nature. In the Amazon you will discover Tree Frogs, Piranha Fish and electric eels. In the Rainforest you will be amazed at the Armadillo and the Toucan. In the blistering heat of the African Savannah you will come across Lions and elephants and hyenas. And you will discover how God is at work in these amazing environments.

Amazon Adventures by Horace Banner
ISBN 978-1-85792-440-4
African Adventures by Dick Anderson
ISBN 978-1-85792-807-5
Great Barrier Reef Adventures by Jim Cromarty
ISBN 978-1-84550-068-9
Himalayan Adventures by Penny Reeve
ISBN 978-1-84550-080-1
Kiwi Adventures by Bartha Hill
ISBN 978-1-84550-282-9
Outback Adventures by Jim Cromarty
ISBN 978-1-85792-974-4
Rainforest Adventures by Horace Banner
ISBN 978-1-85792-627-9
Rocky Mountain Adventures by Betty Swinford
ISBN 978-1-85792-962-1
Scottish Highland Adventures by Catherine Mackenzie
ISBN 978-1-84550-281-2
Wild West Adventures by Donna Vann
ISBN 978-1-84550-065-8

NOTES

NOTES

NOTES

NOTES

NOTES

NOTES

CHRISTIAN FOCUS PUBLICATIONS

Christian Focus | Christian Heritage | CF4K | Mentor

Christian Focus Publications publishes books for adults and children under its four main imprints: Christian Focus, Christian Heritage, CF4K and Mentor. Our books reflect that God's word is reliable and Jesus is the way to know him, and live for ever with him.

Our children's publication list includes a Sunday School curriculum that covers pre-school to early teens; puzzle and activity books. We also publish personal and family devotional titles, biographies and inspirational stories that children will love.

If you are looking for quality Bible teaching for children then we have an excellent range of Bible story and age specific theological books.

From pre-school to teenage fictions, we have it covered.

Find us at our web page:
www.christianfocus.com

Reformation Heritage Books

2919 Leonard St, NE, Grand Rapids, MI, 49525
Phone: 616-977-0599; Fax: 616-285-3246
email: orders@heritagebooks.org
Website: www.heritagebooks.org